Penguin Books
A Family Affair

Michael Innes is the pseudonym of J. I. M.
Stewart, who has been Student of Christ Church,
Oxford, since 1949. He was born in 1906 and
was educated at Edinburgh Academy and Oriel
College, Oxford. He was lecturer in English
at the University of Leeds from 1930 to 1935,
when he became Jury Professor of English in the
University of Adelaide, South Australia. From
1946 to 1948 he was Lecturer in English at
Queen's University, Belfast. He has published
books on English literature and novels under his
own name, as well as detective novels and
broadcast scripts as Michael Innes.
He is married and has five children.

'A Family Affair – Appleby junior, brilliant Oxford undergraduate son of the noted sleuths becomes 'tec in his turn and helps his father (and mother) to rumble a set of amusing hoaxes. Who posed as Sir Joshua Reynolds and fooled a rich meat-merchant into thinking he could paint his wife's portrait? Written with all Mr Innes's skill and wit' – *Sunday Telegraph*

'Appleby of the Yard now lamentably retired turns his idle hands to the puzzle of the recurring art hoaxes, as introduced by his son Bobby and young Oxford accomplices. The complicated, ingenious mystery is pure Innes with plenty of laughs and mental exercise for those inclined' – *Liverpool Daily Post*

Michael Innes

A Family Affair

Penguin Books

Penguin Books Ltd, Harmondsworth,
Middlesex, England
Penguin Books Australia Ltd, Ringwood,
Victoria, Australia

First published by Victor Gollancz 1969
Published in Penguin Books 1972
Copyright © Michael Innes, 1969

Made and printed in Great Britain by
C. Nicholls & Company Ltd
Set in Intertype Plantin

Part One

The Voonderble Vorlt of Art

Chapter One

Bobby Appleby's Oxford life was not altogether an easy one. Providence was responsible. Providence had framed Bobby as an athlete, but had added to this certain mental endowments of which one of the earlier manifestations had been a notably rapid cunning. In a scrum-half nothing is more prizeable than such a combination. Bobby had become a very good scrum-half – despite owning half a dozen more inches (and perhaps a couple of dozen more pounds) than very good scrum-halves are commonly endowed with. Bobby, in fact, even when crouched beside a scrum, couldn't avoid the appearance of towering over it, and all his days this had lent an embarrassing suggestion of comedy to his appearances on the Rugger field. But for the challenge which this physical disparity (and the amusement it occasioned) presented, Bobby might have got clear of the game on leaving school. As it was, he had gone on playing it, and in due course had gained his Blue.

But, lurkingly at least, Bobby was an intellectual. His tutors knew that he would put up a good show in Schools, and only wondered how good it would be. And in his final year this brainy bent was no longer to be concealed. Bobby continued to go about with clumps of muscular characters, who puffed and sweated and had mud behind their ears. But he also went about with the cleverest young men in the college. And it was a college in which the cleverest young men were reputed to be very clever indeed.

Living thus between divided and disparted worlds required a certain amount of tact and flexibility. For one thing, the worlds *were* divided and disparted. In Bobby's father's time juvenile Oxford had been divided into hearties, aesthetes, and unobtrusive youths commonly known as the sub-men. Since then, the words had changed, and perhaps the categories had a little shifted as well. The sub-men had become grey men, and occasionally showed alarming streaks of colour. The aesthetes might be said virtually to have vanished from the scene, since nobody would have been gratified by the appellation, and only the ineradicable conservatism of undergraduate journalism kept the word in being at all; still, an inclination to the arts lingered here and there. One would have had to say, at least, that aesthetes had diminished as compared with another category – one hardly known in Bobby's father's time, but perfectly well known in his grandfather's. Bobby's grandfather would have called them the reading men – and it was they, of course, whom the newspapers called intellectuals. The hearties, although qualitatively much as before (only the word, again, had become rather old-hat), were a dwindling race numerically. In fact there seemed to be rather a strong current of feeling among the young that organized games, if proper at all, were proper only for the younger still. So there was something slightly embattled and defensive about those who still believed that an honourable number of boats should be propelled up and down the river, and that fifteens and elevens ought to be fielded as required. Bobby Appleby didn't find moving in and out of this fortress altogether easy.

Sir John Appleby, although by no means an intrusive parent, was sufficiently aware of this situation to be interested in it. Bobby was his youngest child; in the others it was harder and harder to detect any sign that they were still growing up; Bobby's progress was the more in focus as a result. Nothing but amusement was involved, since Bobby seemed not remotely likely to become in any substantial way an odd man out. Still, perhaps a couple of times a term, Appleby and his wife would motor up to Oxford and have lunch with Bobby at the Mitre, or tea in his rooms. That sort of thing. Bobby employed these occasions for the purpose of affording his parents a pre-view of friends whom he proposed bringing home in vacations. Rough shooting or beagling, or a proposal to read together the *Choephoroe* or the *Trachiniae*, would be discussed with equal gravity. It was all rather well-behaved, and the young gentlemen would treat Judith Appleby as if she were a duchess with Edwardian views. These occasions were entertaining, all the same.

But this occasion was different. It was a dinner *en garçon* –

although the members of the dining club (which was called, indeed, the Patriarchs) might not have cared for its being so described. Bobby had recently become a member of the Patriarchs. Following a custom which was understood to be of immemorial antiquity, the Patriarchs had then invited Bobby's father to dine as a guest of the club. One doesn't have to make speeches at an affair like the Patriarchs. So here Appleby was.

The Patriarchs had dined in a common room which Appleby supposed to have been borrowed for the occasion from yet graver persons; at least it was an apartment hideously hung with fading photographs of whiskery Victorian dons. But now they had adjourned to the rooms of a member who appeared to have taken on the duties of host, and who dispensed port with gravity. When all had been thus accommodated, the company rose to the toast of Church and King. Appleby, reflecting on 'King' rather than 'Queen', concluded that the Patriarchs must attribute to themselves some vaguely Jacobite persuasion. But his host was now producing an out-size candle in an out-size candlestick (the latter, Appleby suspected, sacrilegiously purloined from the college chapel), and upon this the members advanced one by one for the purpose of lighting cigars. They made a very deep bow to the candle – which was something savouring, surely, a little too much of idolatry for the original biblical patriarchs to have approved of. After these ritual solemnities, the young men became entirely natural again. Appleby wasn't sure that Bobby hadn't felt rather a fool behaving in this way under the eye of a parent. But at least he had seen his father perform the rite with the most unflawed decorum.

The port was excellent. It must also be expensive, and Appleby noticed that there was a crate of beer under a table. He resolved to leave before the beer. But that would be a long time off, and he hoped in the meantime to enjoy quite a lot of the Patriarchs' conversation. It was rather sparing at the moment – perhaps because they were nervous about their cigars going out. If that happened, you were probably required to go through the business with the candle again. He looked round at the assembled youths. Their complexions, fair and clear, were almost as uniform as their dinner-jackets. But some wore their hair very long, and the conjunction of this with evening clothes had the odd effect of seeming to withdraw them by a century or more from the modern scene; they might have been contemporaries of Tennyson's or Thackeray's (only that would be at Cambridge) conscientiously entertaining themselves at what used to be called a wine. *My dear Mama, I hope you are well. Tennyson of Trinity gave a wine last night. It was mostly serious men who were there, and I enjoyed it very much. An Etonian called Hallam, rather senior to the rest of us, introduced the theme of Religious Doubt. Tennyson has become quite a "swell" (our new word, Mama), having won a medal for a poem about Timbuctoo . . .*

Appleby jerked himself out of this fantasy, since to lose himself in it would be uncivil. Besides, a further stage in the evening's proceedings had been reached. The President of the Patriarchs was calling upon a certain Paddy Moyle (who had been looking nervous for some time) to "introduce a topic".

And at this the assembled Patriarchs assumed expressions of severe attention. Appleby, without any difficulty, did the same.

Mr Moyle's topic proved to be 'Practical Jokes'. This at least gave promise of more liveliness than 'Religious Doubt', even although – as it turned out – Mr Moyle started off from Holy Writ. What, he asked the company, was the first practical joke? He was inclined to give his own vote to the Flood. Flood switched on; Flood switched off; roars of laughter in heaven. This was the very type, the very archetype, of practical joking.

A tall youth sitting next to Bobby (of a privileged class of society, clearly, since he was having no difficulty with his cigar at all) interrupted to disagree. God had contrived a much earlier practical joke than *that*. Think of the first sunset! Adam pottering complacently round his new estate, not much noticing what was going on in the sky. Then the whole thing faded out on him, and in no time he couldn't see a yard in front of his nose. Think of the shivering despair in which the poor devil passed the night! But morning arrived, and the Prime Orb bobbed up again. Heaven's laughter must have been very loud indeed. Top practical joke.

'But hadn't Eve already been created?' Bobby asked. 'She was a pretty stiff joke at the innocent Adam's expense, wasn't she? Think of Marvell. "Two paradises 'twere in one, To live in Paradise alone".'

'Talking of the Flood,' somebody said, rather belatedly. 'There's a practical joke about it in Chaucer. The first recorded English practical joke. It's in *The Reeve's Tale,* isn't it?'

'*The Miller's Tale,* you ignoramus,' Mr Moyle said. Mr Moyle was becoming a little impatient to get on with his own remarks.

'That's right. One chap is persuaded to spend the night in a tub hoisted up to the rafters, because they tell him there's going to be another Flood. It enables another chap to sleep with his wife. In the end, he's cut down with a crash. Uproarious, wouldn't you say?'

'At least a *practical* joke,' Bobby pointed out. 'Joker gets wench. Some point to the thing.'

This remark excited a ribaldry not at all inhibited by the presence of the Patriarchs' elderly guest. It was against the background of this that Mr Moyle had to assert himself.

'That's what I want to go on to,' he said. 'Why they're called practical jokes. I don't think it has anything to do with the deception paying a dividend, as in Chaucer's story. Think of the most rudimentary kind, that you can buy in squalid little shops for a shilling. Something you put on the floor or the table, to pretend the ink's been spilt or the cat's been sick. There are more ingenious ones that are quite revolting. Their purpose is to disgust or frighten or humiliate. The basis of the ploy is always essentially malicious.'

'I say – talking of Chaucer.' It was the man who had harked back to the Flood who now harked back again. 'There's a story by Rudyard Kipling called "Dayspring Mishandled". It's about somebody spending years and years first forging and then planting a Chaucer manuscript, just in order to fool and discredit another scholar, who is supposed to be frightfully disagreeable. At least, it's something like that. And I think a practical joke might really be defined as applied satire. The castigation of folly, and all that. Sadism – and malice, as Paddy says – masquerading as moral zeal. But I still don't understand the word "practical".'

'You will if you let me get on to it,' Mr Moyle said with some warmth. 'As a matter of fact, it seems to me quite an interesting bit of semantics. And it hasn't been remarked hitherto, so far as I can discover.'

'Mr Moyle's essays,' someone said in a don's voice, 'may be relied upon for an air of making a contribution to their subject.'

'Machination,' Mr Moyle said, ignoring this. 'In the sixteenth century, a "practice" is a stratagem directed at an evil end. And the adjective was used in the same way. So that's what a practical joke is. A crafty one.'

'Do we understand,' Bobby asked, 'that the expression "practical joke" is known to have been current in a period when "practical" could still mean "crafty"?'

'Not exactly.' Mr Moyle appeared slightly at a loss for a moment, but then recovered confidence. 'However,' he added, 'the use may doubtless be inferred.'

'Don't the best practical jokes tend to be disinterested?' Appleby asked. It was plain that the Patriarchs' guest must utter in the course of the evening.

'Do you mean without a victim, sir?' somebody said. 'I don't see that that's possible.'

'Well, I admit that a practical joke is always, broadly speaking, a hoax; and that in any hoax there has to be somebody to be taken in. But it need scarcely be a specific somebody. Swinburne – at least, I think it was Swinburne – once invented an obscure French poet – I believe it was a poet – and published a substantial essay on him. The victim was something quite vague; say, the literary world at large. Or there were the people who dressed up as navvies and dug an enormous hole in the middle of Bond Street. Or think of some of the most famous impersonations carried off by practical jokers. More often than not, any element of malice was minimal in them.'

'A joke may be disinterested,' Mr Moyle said. 'But it can't be unmotivated. And that's what I rather wanted to go on to: what may be called the psychology of the joker. I have come to the conclusion that the typical practical joker labours under a sense of inferiority and insecurity. So he has to prove himself sharper-witted than other people. For example, there was a real man not long ago who forged things rather as that scholar in Kipling's story does.'

'T. J. Wise,' somebody said.

'That's right. He was quite a well-heeled business gent with cultivated interests. He collected books in a big way, with the result that he was much run after by scholars. But he wasn't himself a scholar. I don't think he'd even had the kind of education that is the privilege of everybody in this room.'

'A deprivation painful to think of,' the Patriarchs' host of the evening said. He was still going conscientiously round with the port.

'As a consequence, Wise inclined to feel these learned hangers-on really had a patronizing attitude to him. So he did all his forgeries, and took all these chaps in. Probably they hadn't really been laughing at him at all. But he felt they had. And now – without their knowing it – he was in a position to laugh at them.'

'He sounds a bit of a special case to me,' Bobby said. 'I don't believe many people would respond with practical jokes to some embittered sense that they hadn't themselves made a grade. Wasn't there a chap who hired the Oxford Town Hall, and gave a very successful lecture in the character of some eminent continental philosopher? I don't believe for a moment that he was a failed philosopher himself. He was from some quite different walk of life, and just out for a little quiet fun.'

'Isn't this whole topic one of merely antiquarian interest?' A fresh voice asked this from the back of the room. It belonged to a young man who was reclining in an armchair with a great air of elderly ease. 'Think of rags, for instance. You mayn't even know what I mean. Not what the Welfare State compels undergraduates to dress in, but how they used to behave when feeling a bit bored. Just doesn't happen nowadays. Has any of you ever *seen* a rag taking place?'

'Perhaps not here,' the man with the decanter said. 'But the Redbrick places have rags. They're usually on a day appointed in advance by a Vice-Chancellor or somebody. Rather pitiful. Running about in fancy dress, kidnapping gratified leading citizens in aid of charity.'

'But that isn't a real rag,' somebody protested. 'And I don't know that even real rags have much to do with practical jokes. Dictionary, please.' A fat volume was promptly pitched across the room, and the speaker fielded it neatly. He flicked through its pages. 'Here you are. The *O.E.D.* gives, as you might expect, very much a don's definition. "Rag: an extensive display of noisy disorderly conduct, carried on in defiance of authority or discipline." Distinctly hostile, wouldn't you say? And the same with the verb. "To rag: to annoy, tease, torment; specially in University slang, to assail in a rough or noisy fashion." No element of wit allowed in a rag. So the rag and the practical joke are distinct species, as I said.'

'I don't think that's quite true.' Mr Moyle, who had plainly done his prep. and had a good deal more learning to unload, was again impatient. 'Practical jokes requiring a lot of team-work tend to have the character of rags. And Oswyn over there is mistaken in thinking that such things no longer happen in Oxford. Only a few years ago, just before our time, some obscure college or other – I forget which – woke up to find its hall transformed in the night. It had been turfed all over, planted with shrubs and flowers, provided with a sparkling little stream from a fire-hydrant, and generously populated with feathered songsters of the grove. And everything had been brought in over the roof, so the organization must have been first-class. I'd say the scale of the thing made it a rag.'

There was a moment's silence. The Patriarchs appeared not greatly stimulated by this purely lexicographical aspect of their subject. Moreover the port was running low, and Appleby began to think about his departure. With the beer, he suspected, would come a change of key. The Patriarchs probably ended these symposia with rude balladry and the improvising of improper songs. It turned out, however, that the moment for anything of the sort had not quite come. The tall youth called Oswyn had sunk yet further back in his chair. But from this position he suddenly spoke in a voice that dominated the room.

'I must tell you about something that happened to my father,' Oswyn said. 'But in more spacious days. In fact, donkeys' ages ago.'

Chapter Two

From the attentive silence which had fallen upon the company, it was apparent that the youth whose Christian name (as it presumably was) was Oswyn enjoyed a reputation as a raconteur. And he at once displayed his command of this character by a little deferring expectation. He did this by extricating himself gracefully from his chair, crossing the room with his port glass in his hand, and sitting down beside Appleby. Perhaps he thought Bobby's father so old that he was probably rather deaf, or perhaps he simply felt that what he had to say should, as a matter of politeness, be given the appearance of being offered to the club's guest in the first place. And he began by asking Appleby a question.

'Would you say, sir, that what we're talking about – practical jokes and so on – had a kind of golden age in the Edwardian period?'

'I think that is probably so.' Appleby wondered whether he ought to disclaim any personal memory of such goings on at the turn of the century. 'And I'm not sure that there wasn't a silver age rather later on. Quite sophisticated people sometimes evolved jokes which no doubt seem childish now.' Appleby looked meditatively at the outsize candle. 'To appear in any degree *pas sérieux* seems not at all the thing in your generation. Take Bobby, for example. Unlike Max's Matthew Arnold, Bobby is invariably wholly serious. And I observe the same characteristic, if I may say so, in the membership of your club as a whole.'

Appleby found that his glass was being hastily replenished. The Patriarchs had taken this banter rather well. It was what they expected in a guest of great age.

'For instance,' Oswyn was saying, 'there were the people who dressed up as the Shah of Persia and his *entourage* – or as something like that – and managed to inspect a battleship.'

'Yes, indeed,' Appleby said. 'And they included one of Leslie Stephen's girls.'

'My father means Virginia Woolf,' Bobby said a shade grimly.

'That's right,' Oswyn agreed. 'And it was the kind of thing that happened to my father. He's an old-fashioned character, by the way. And we're landed with rather a large house, you know. A useless great place, crammed with every sort of junk. Bobby, isn't that right? You've been and had a look at us.'

'Entirely right,' Bobby said. 'Lywards must have been magpies for generations.'

Appleby noted the name. It rang some sort of bell. A muted *Field* or *Country Life* sort of bell. The youth called Oswyn, he conjectured, must be Lord Oswyn Lyward.

'Different sorts of magpie,' Oswyn said, 'from generation to generation. Some quite early ones were pretty hot, I'd say. Tended to find themselves possessed of bits and pieces by Cellini –'

'Cellini?' somebody interrupted with interest. 'Didn't he write a dirty book?'

'Very moderately so, Robin. You're probably thinking of Casanova. Bits and pieces by Cellini, as I was saying, or a few nice little family miniatures by Nicholas Hilliard. But then we'd revert to type – you people must stop me if I get boring in a family way – and accumulate the most frightful things – or at least the just-not-good-enough things. My great-grandfather, for instance, went in for Etty.'

'Etty's all right,' somebody protested. 'I'd like an Etty.'

'My dear Charles, a nude lady by Etty, belly-forward and standing chastely in the middle of a waterfall, is *not* the same thing as a nude lady by Boucher, splayed bottom-up on a sofa. *Sancta simplicitas.*'

'*Mais tous les deux,*' Bobby murmured, '*ont senti la chair.*'

'Isn't this rather losing direction?' Mr Moyle asked.

'Only because Bobby's showing off,' Oswyn said. 'Anyway, the point is that my father, unlike quite a number of my family a bit nearer to Noah's Ark, is no sort of *virtuoso* or *curioso*. He spent a lot of time in India, you know, but his morals were at least wholly uncorrupted by all that shocking sculpture and so on. He went out with a simple taste for shooting, and with a simple taste for shooting he returned.'

'Natives?' the host of the evening asked with serious interest. 'I mean, was it one of the periods for that sort of thing?'

'Not in the least. My father was extravagantly liberal-minded and humane. He simply went into jungles and places in a big way, and shot all sorts of lions and tigers. He brought them home – either stuffed or decapitated or flattened out as rugs – and we have them all over the place. Not that they have much to do with what I'm telling you. They just serve to sketch in my father.'

'Is he what is called a backwoods peer?' somebody asked politely.

'Yes, that's exactly him. And it's an important part of the story, as a matter of fact. You see, in spite of India and all that, my father has never much taken up with people. Hardly ever goes to Town, really. Always been very much one for the private life. He did High Sheriff once, and found it awful. Particularly the Assize Judges. Old gentlemen dressed up like Father Christmas, and hanging people right and left. They never did that in India, he says. As for Lord Lieutenant, he turned it down flat, although it created a bit of a stink. Family always *has* done the job, I suppose. But he just said wandering royalty would be a bit too much. Not what you might call a Buck House type, my father. That's where the story begins, as a matter of fact.'

'We perceive,' the man who had been interested in Cellini said, 'that we are to make an incursion into high life.'

'Pretty dubious high life, as you'll hear in a minute.' Oswyn turned to Appleby. 'I don't know, sir, if you've ever taken time off to look at the amateur side of your job – Sherlock Holmes, and all that?'

'I think I know my Holmes pretty well.' Appleby was amused by this reference to his career. 'But I'm not so good on his successors.'

'Well, it's Holmes I'm thinking of. You remember how, every now and then, he'd receive an emissary from an Exalted Personage, who would ask him to save the Empire, or preserve the reputation of a Personage more Exalted still. And finally Watson would ask him where he'd been one day. And he'd produce a pair of diamond cuff-links, and murmur modestly that he'd been to Windsor, and received them from the hand of a Very Gracious Lady. That sort of thing.'

'That *sort* of thing,' Appleby said. 'Although I doubt whether your account quite measures up to the scholarship of the subject.'

'I'm sure you're right. All I'm saying, really, is that it was a Very Gracious Lady who came at my father. Of course she's dead now, God rest her soul. My father simply had a telephone message that she was coming to tea. At Keynes, that is. Keynes is the name of our house.'

'Quite out of the blue?' somebody asked.

'Entirely. But there was nothing odd about it. My father and mother were quite proper people to hand the muffins and pour the fragrant Lapsang in such circumstances.'

'Muffins?' Mr Moyle asked curiously. 'Would there really be –'

'Well, whatever Very Gracious Ladies do consume. This one had a fancy for going round people's houses. And she had rather a vexatious habit as well.'

'A notion,' Appleby said, 'of what should appropriately mark such an occasion.'

'Just that, sir. She had old-fashioned ideas, just as my father had. It seems that well into the eighteenth century, at least, a visitor whom one desired to distinguish was always given anything he fancied to take away. A volume from your library – that sort of thing. There are shocking gaps, it seems, in some libraries of importance, just because of this habit. My father's august guest kept this up in quite a big way. It was a kind of joke, it seems, among the sort of people who were likely to suffer from it. Everybody knew about it – or nearly everybody. I'm not sure about my father. He's a person who lives rather remote from gossip, and so on.

'Well, the circus arrived. All very much in order: police escort, Rolls, equerry, lady-in-waiting – the entire works. I think my mother was quite pleased; she didn't dislike the notion of her bun-fight figuring in the Court Circular next morning. The Very Gracious Lady seemed to have a bad cold, but the occasion went swimmingly, all the same. Only, she didn't stay very long.'

'Ah!' Appleby said.

'She was a good deal taken with the Hilliards, but as they are ancestors she couldn't very well make improper suggestions about them. What she *did* declare herself enchanted with – what she *much* envied my father the possession of – was some odd little daub, about twelve inches square, which I expect he was hardly aware of the existence of. But that was that. India, of course, had made him pretty good at taking a hint. He yanked the thing from the wall, rather annoyed my mother by blowing a lot of dust from it, and handed it to the equerry. The chap had the drill pat: two steps forward, receive picture, two steps back. Conclusion of visit.'

'And the next morning,' Appleby said, 'there was nothing in the Court Circular?'

'Nothing at all. Nor was there a letter the next day. My father, as a matter of fact, is rather a stickler in such things – India again, I suppose – and he wasn't pleased. A letter from the Private Secretary, it seems, is *de rigueur* on such occasions –'

'And a signed photograph?' somebody asked. 'Or do they go only to the middle classes?'

'Probably a signed photograph as well.' Oswyn was not offended. 'So my father wrote in, expressing the loyal hope that the V.G.L.'s cold was none the worse for her trip. Well, there was a chap down from London in no time, dead keen that the whole hoax should be kept mum.'

'It *was* a hoax?' Mr Moyle asked.

'Of course it was a hoax. And one just like the inspecting of that battleship. The type of the purely disinterested practical joke that Sir John was talking about.'

'Only you don't believe it *was* disinterested,' Appleby said. 'Your narrative has emphasized something it was meant to emphasize. The little daub.'

'That's perfectly true, sir. Ever since I was told the story, I have rather wondered about the small picture.'

'And your father – hasn't he wondered?'

'I just don't know. But I rather think not.'

'I see.' Appleby looked curiously at the young man who had entertained the Patriarchs to so odd a tale. 'But simple curiosity would surely prompt one to inquire? There must be a catalogue,

21

an inventory, records from the last occasion upon which death duties were paid –'

Perfectly politely, Oswyn interrupted this with a low laugh.

'You should come and have a look at us,' he said. 'My parents would be delighted. You must have Bobby bring you.'

'That would be very pleasant.' Appleby was aware of a stir among the Patriarchs, and of the beer crate being tugged from beneath the table. 'But this is very much a matter of past history?'

'Yes, of course.' Oswyn was airily vague. 'Donkeys' ages ago, as I said. Such things don't happen nowadays.'

Appleby said good-night to Bobby outside the Master's Lodging. The quad was filled with a faintly luminous yellow fog, as if some giant hand had ladled into it an unpalatably dilute pea-soup. There was a faint smell, deceptively rural, of sodden leaves. A piano was being played in a farther quad, but the notes came without resonance, as if through wet flannel. Somewhere a great bell began to sound, and then many lesser bells. The piano ceased abruptly, suggesting that it must be in the proprietorship of someone of nervously law-abiding disposition. The big bell stopped decisively, and then the little bells rather at random. Appleby opened the door of the Lodging, and went in.

The Master was reading Plato in his library, with a tall glass and a whisky-decanter as his only aids. It must be wonderful, Appleby thought, not to require a Liddell and Scott. The Master pushed the decanter absent-mindedly forward. He had not the air of one politely waiting up for a wandering guest.

'I hope I didn't stay too long, or leave too early,' Appleby said.

'You could scarcely have achieved the former, I imagine, so far as the young men were concerned.' The Master didn't seem to have given much thought to the evolving of this courtesy; the *Parmenides,* a teasing affair, takes some emerging from. 'I forget,' he said. 'Was it the Rugger Club?'

'It was the Patriarchs.'

'To be sure. I recall that your son is the Great Amphibian of his year. I was a Patriarch myself once. Conceivably I am still their Senior Member. But, guests apart, there is an age-limit on actual attendance.' The Master closed his Oxford Classical Text a shade reluctantly. 'Very pleasant lads,' he said.

'Yes, indeed.' Appleby saw no reason to dissent from this urbane judgement. At the same time he wondered whether there could ever be any conceivable group of young men of whom the Master would say briskly 'Scruffy little tykes' or 'Idle and insolent parasites'. 'A boy called Oswyn Lyward,' Appleby went on, as he poured himself a token whisky, 'told us an amusing story of a hoax played on his father.'

'Ah, the Very Gracious Lady!'

'You've heard of her?'

'Lyward told me the story on, I think, the third occasion of his lunching with me. Just the right stage, wouldn't you say, for an undergraduate to launch out on quite a stretch of narrative?'

'No doubt.' Appleby wondered irreverently whether the younger sons of marquises got invited to lunch in the Lodging more frequently than commoner commoners. 'Do you know his father?'

'Slightly.' The Master tossed his book on a table and rose to attend hospitably to the fire. 'The worthy Lord Cockayne is an old member of the college, and turns up at a Gaudy or the like from time to time. He's getting on. Oswyn is the youngest child.' The Master turned from the fireplace to glance at his guest in benign amusement. 'My dear Appleby, I believe you are taking a professional interest in the lad's story. A trick of the old rage, is it not?'

'Perhaps so.' Appleby put down his glass. 'Such as it has been, you see, my career as a copper began in a college just across the High. The affair of poor President Umpleby.'

'To be sure. Peace to his bones.'

'There were rather a lot of bones, as a matter of fact. His study had virtually the character of an ossuary.'

'Is that so? The details escape my memory. But he was my tutor, of course. We once made a trip up the Rhine together. It was the thing to do. But I seem to remember he was to be given an honorary degree at Bonn. Very much at random, often, the distribution of these things. He was no scholar, poor man, although as a tutor he was well enough. What were we talking about?'

'The small painting carried off from Keynes Court. Or at least we were coming round to it. Being stolen property, it has its legitimate interest for me as an ex-policeman.'

'Wasn't it all rather a long time ago? The young man himself surely has no recollection of it?'

'I don't think he has. He was rather vague, but it was my impression that he was, as yet, either unborn or still in his well-sprung aristocratic pram.'

'The latter, I'd guess. But we can readily arrive at the *terminus ad quem*.' The Master moved over to a bookcase. 'All we need is the appropriate volume of *Who Was Who*. And this will be it. We want the year of the V.G.L.'s death. Deplorable that one doesn't carry in one's head notable dates of that sort.' The Maser's practised fingers turned the pages rapidly. 'Here we are. The Royal Personage in question died in 1950. The episode certainly occurred before Oswyn had passed from his nanny to his governess.'

'And rather before stealing pictures from great houses became really fashionable.' Appleby got to his feet. 'What we are confronting is a pioneer operation.'

'You fascinate me. But can you be quite sure? I mean, that the picture was of any importance? As a crime, if you will forgive my saying so, the affair strikes me as totally fantastic. As a practical joke, it is another matter. Might not there have been a wager involved? May not the spurious V.G.L. have undertaken to "bring off" – I imagine that would be the term – the triumphant carrying away of some object totally without value? Only persons with a certain position in the world – or at least of a certain sophistication – could hope to bring off this particular hoax successfully. I can imagine their giving great care precisely to *not* asking the innocent Marquis of Cockayne for anything that could possibly have monetary value.'

'That, Master, if I may say so, is a most cogent observation. Still, one doesn't quite know.'

'And there's another thing. Oswyn Lyward, as I remember him, gives a most amusing account of Keynes Court as a gigantic lumber-room. But it can't really be so. Such places have librarians and other semi-learned persons who know all about everything, wouldn't you say? What *could* this little picture be, that the people of that sort – and lawyers and so on, if it had any value – didn't know of?'

'Almost anything.' Appleby, who was about to say good night, spoke with confidence. 'We come here, Master, to something I know about. What can lurk unknown in a place like Keynes Court is quite incredible. What about, say, Raphael?'

'Raphael!'

'Early on, he was rather fond of doing panels about twelve inches square. Think of the little St George and the Dragon –'

'Forgive me, my dear fellow – but what exactly *is* a Raphael? Philosophically or metaphysically regarded, I grant you, it is an artifact brought into being – on wood or canvas, and with the aid of brushes and pigments – by a certain Raphael Sanzio, who died, I believe, round about 1520. But, in practical and pragmatic terms, what is a Raphael? Surely it is a similar artifact, which happens to have a reputable provenance connecting it with this particular painter? The notion that there are persons called "experts", who can look at an artifact with *no* provenance and say "Raphael" with authority –'

'You are quite wrong, Master.' Appleby was amused. 'All that may be absent is *certainty*. And that goes, really, for many things with a most impeccable provenance: detailed description by Vasari, say, and a chain of known owners from that day to this. *Authority* is another matter. There is quite enough of it around to establish an *unknown* Raphael as an *authentic* Raphael. A favourable expertise by the right people, and the job is done. So postulate a thief who happens to know that Lord Cockayne owns a Raphael which nobody has thought of as a Raphael – or really so much as noticed – for hundreds of years. He at once knows something else as well: that if he can lay his hands on it, and invent some harmless story as to how the obscure thing came into his possession, he has possessed himself of something which he can part with for tens of thousands of pounds.'

'And, in this case, he did the parting, we must suppose, nearly twenty years ago. It makes, surely, rather a cold trail?'

'Yes, indeed. But – do you know? – from a professional or

technical point of view, a cold trail can be more absorbing than a hot one.' Appleby took a step forward and tapped the *Parmenides*. 'I almost remember,' he said. 'Is it the forms that Plato is shooting at? Or is it the sensibles? A cold trail, surely. But here you are, Master, sitting up with it.'

'But not any longer tonight.' And the Master moved to the door of his library. 'Shall we meet for breakfast at nine?'

Chapter Three

'But, John,' Judith Appleby said incredulously, 'you can't possibly propose simply to go and *investigate*!'

'I don't see why not. Of course, it would have to be with Bobby's sanction. But he'd have to know, in any case. The idea was that he would take me there.'

'The young man must have been speaking quite idly. Think of it. You walk in on this unoffending and elderly nobleman –'

'I'm elderly myself.'

'Not so elderly as *that*. And you recall to him that, years and years ago, he was made a complete fool of, and that you have turned up at Keynes Court for the purpose of poking around. I think he'd probably set the dogs on you.'

'That's what he ought to have done to his bogus royal visitor. But Lord Cockayne won't *think* of it as all that long ago. The years telescope themselves, you know, in the memory of the old. And the thing will always have rankled with him. He'll be glad to have the scoundrels caught up with. And I'm rather *like* Holmes, after all. Or is it like Wilkie Collins's Sergeant Cuff? Accustomed to conducting myself respectfully but firmly among my betters. Besides, I must know quite a number of the old gentleman's cronies. I expect we'll get along swimmingly.'

'There's the pruning.'

'So there is.' Appleby appeared much struck by this consideration. 'But wouldn't Hoobin be quite good at that?'

'Let Hoobin loose on the new cordons with the sécateurs!' Lady Appleby's tone expressed absolute outrage. 'I shall have to do the whole job myself. How bored you are, John, with country life. Like your wretched Holmes with his bees.'

'He wasn't. He doated on them. And I doat on Hoobin.' Appleby got up from the breakfast-table, walked to the window, and gazed out over the garden of Dream Manor. 'Odd that you should have inherited the place. But I do entirely approve of it.'

'I'm delighted to hear you say so.' Judith glanced suspiciously at her husband as he turned back into the room. 'John, is there something more in this than you've told me?'

'It's just possible there is.' Appleby was now quite serious. 'The affair puts me in mind of one of the accounts I never closed. There were plenty of them, you know. At the Yard there's a whole filing-cabinet full of them.'

'I don't believe it. Your career there was almost indecently successful. And now you've become very good at pruning fruit-trees too.'

'Really?' There was honest surprise in Appleby's voice. 'Perhaps I'd better not go off on a wild-goose chase, after all. I'll just tip some old colleague a wink. A retired man does look rather foolish harking back after –'

'You know very well I'm saying nothing of that kind. I don't think you ought to duck out of this.'

'Duck out of it!' For a moment this tergiversation left Appleby speechless. 'Explain yourself. Clarify your attitude.'

'"His helmet now shall be a hive for bees." Doesn't some Elizabethan poet say something like that? Why should you hang your helmet on the peg – just because London's traffic problems and call-girls and casinos proved boring? If there's something in this that might be *fun* –'

'I'll go up to Town tomorrow,' Appleby said.

'My dear chap, it's so extremely nice to see you.' The grey-haired Commissioner with the weary wrinkles round his eyes – he was not, in fact, much younger than Appleby – looked at once warily and with genuine cordiality at his almost legendary visitor. 'And if you've dropped in professionally, so to speak, that's all the better fun, I'd say.'

'Fun?' Appleby appeared to catch some echo in the word. 'You must tell me at once if I'm just being irresponsible. But you see what has come into my head. This Keynes Court affair was ages ago. But it does fit in with an odd series of reports. Away back at that time, I mean. But what if that sort of thing has been continuing? It was, as I see it, an uncommonly good line. The victim has been made ridiculous – and at the same time the extent of his material loss isn't all that clear to him. So he keeps mum – or at least he plays the thing down. There's even a refinement in Cockayne's case. It's put to him fairly firmly that publicizing the foible of an august personage –'

'Her magpie instinct,' the Commissioner said encouragingly.

'Just that. Making a fuss about it wouldn't be the thing. Let's keep mum, and call it a day.'

'I doubt whether just the same trick could be played twice. And certainly there's no record of anything of the kind.'

'Oh, quite. And the formula – if there was, and is, a formula – is much more generalized. It's simply the disinterested joke or hoax which, if peered into, would prove not all that disinterested, after all. There was something in it for somebody. You see? Perhaps it's extravagant to speak of a series. I have only two incidents in my head.'

'The Carrington Stubbs?' The Commissioner, who had glanced at a paper, was again encouraging. 'An awkward family affair, and no apparent damage done. So it was dropped.'

'That was one of them. I never felt we'd really tied it up. You've looked at the file? A decent country squire, with the family's favourite hunters and gun-dogs and whatever over several generations hanging cheek by jowl with deceased Carringtons on the walls. When George Stubbs became fashionable, Sir Thomas Carrington became dimly convinced he owned a Stubbs. And the Royal Academy held some sort of Eighteenth Century show –'

'And their secretary wrote to Carrington –' The Commissioner broke off, and chuckled. 'Only he hadn't written at all, really, because there had been some sort of hoax –'

'Just that. But Carrington packed off what he believed to be his Stubbs –'

'Exactly. And there was an accident – or was it a maniac with a little hatchet? Anyway, the picture had actually been hung, and somehow it was damaged, and Sir Thomas was very angry. So the restorers got going, and in no time they found that under Stubbs there was a jolly little painting of the coronation of Edward the Seventh. And Carrington's mother had been an amateur painter, and rather an eccentric character as well –'

'So somebody was felt to have perpetrated a tasteless joke, and it was all hushed up.' Appleby paused. 'But had there been a real Stubbs, and somebody made off with it? Poor Sir Thomas just didn't want to know. Nor was Mr Meatyard at all anxious that the police should too pertinaciously inquire into his meeting with Sir Joshua Reynolds.'

'Oh, come, Appleby!' The Commissioner's incredulity was not unnatural. 'I never heard of that one, my dear fellow. And nobody was ever called Meatyard. It's unbelievable.'

'Not at all. Mr Meatyard was a manufacturer, and no doubt of limited cultivation. But he had an honourable instinct to acquire only the best. He wanted a portrait of his wife, and it appears that he answered some sort of advertisement. A gentleman called on him, and explained that the most eminent of living portrait painters was Sir Joshua Reynolds. Mr Meatyard had *heard* of Sir Joshua, and at once agreed to be accompanied to his studio. But, in order that all should be fair and square, he was advised by the same obliging gentleman to ring up some eminent firm of picture-dealers in Bond Street and inquire the current market price of Reynolds portraits –'

'Nonsense!' The Commissioner threw up his hands. 'I don't believe a word of it!'

'It's absolutely true. Meatyard was a bit staggered by the answer. But he was a wealthy man, and he set out for Sir Joshua's studio. Sir Joshua was extremely affable and accommodating. He fixed up about sittings for Mrs Meatyard, and then he showed Mr Meatyard round his current production line. Mr Meatyard left with a red-hot bargain more or less under his arm. A few days later, Mrs Meatyard rang Sir Joshua's bell. There was, of course, no Sir Joshua. He had, so to speak, returned to the tomb. In a first foolish flush of anger, Mr Meatyard presented himself in this very building. You can look it up, if you want to, in the book. But, in no time, he was soft-pedalling the extent to which he'd been had for a sucker. He'd parted, he said, with a couple of ten-pound notes, and he wanted to take the thing no further. The chronological facts about Sir Joshua Reynolds had been explained to him, and he couldn't face the prospect of his pals roaring with laughter at him at the golf club. Or perhaps on the bowling green. A hoax again, and with ostensibly only an inconsiderable monetary element. But how much did he really part with? We shall never know.'

'Couldn't we find out – and other circumstances of the fraud as well? It ought not really to have been allowed to pass as a practical joke. The worthy man has had a good many years in which to recover from his discomfiture. He might talk about it.'

'I agree. But what I'm hankering after first, you know, is some hint that the racket is still going on. Not all that frequently. Say once in a quinquennium.'

'A hoaxer – or criminal – with a fondness for five-year plans?' The Commissioner nodded thoughtfully. 'It's a field in which continued success would depend on self-restraint. Too many such japes and we'd be alerted to them, wouldn't you say? But any of these three affairs we've been talking about might well yield enough to let the chap rest quite comfortably on his oars for a few years.'

'Or several chaps. The Keynes Court show was quite elaborate. A cavalcade or entourage, you might say.' Rather forgetfully, Appleby had got to his feet and was pacing about the room. He paused at a window and gazed out over the Thames – as he had gazed out over the Thames, through this very window, thousands of times before. The Commissioner watched him benevolently and in silence, but with an expression suggesting that the innocent familiarity pleased him. 'And there's another thing about Keynes Court,' Appleby went on, 'that makes it much the most informative of these enterprising diversions so far. I mean the way it defines itself in social terms. Lord Cockayne mayn't have all that between the ears –'

'Didn't he have a bit of a career somewhere around the Empire? He can't be exactly a moron.'

'Quite so. But what I'm saying is this: even if he *weren't* at all clever, he wouldn't be taken in by *social* impostors. The royal personage, that's to say, and the lady-in-waiting and the equerry or whatever who were tagging after her, must have been impeccably upper class.'

'I suppose so. Yet it's astounding what thoroughly low characters –'

'I know. But not quite in that relation, if you ask me. And, you know, it was rather splendidly *audacious*. Cockayne may by that time have been an established backwoods peer, an aristo-cratic hayseed, if the expression isn't a disrespectful one. But he'd held down jobs which would make the indefinable minutiae of that sort of thing completely familiar to him.'

'Doesn't that suggest that perhaps it *was* a hoax?' The Com-missioner sounded almost hopeful. 'High-spirited frolic by young people belonging to more or less the same world as the Lywards – or whatever the family name is? There's no *proof* that a really *valuable* object was liberated. Nor is there of any pronounced mercenary motive in either of the other two cases.'

'That's partly why I want to find a fourth. And I suppose one ought to look for it in the same general area.' Appleby sud-denly chuckled. 'In what my old friend Braunkopf calls "the voonderble vorlt of art".'

'Braunkopf?' The Commissioner looked up suddenly. 'Not a fellow called – let me think – Hildebert Braunkopf?'

'Yes, indeed.' Appleby was surprised. 'The proprietor of a not very distinguished concern he calls the Da Vinci Gallery. Have his professional occasions been bringing him this way again?'

'Certainly they have – though I'm not clear about the details.' The Commissioner seemed perplexed. 'You say he's a friend of yours – this chap?'

'Say that he was a *protégé* of Judith's at one time.'

'Oh, I see!' The Commissioner was as a man entirely en-lightened.

'And I must say I got rather fond of him myself. So I hope he hasn't really been in trouble. Not that it's unlikely. Braunkopf's a picture-dealer of the utmost enterprise.'

'So far as I know, he was feeling very much the aggrieved party.' The Commissioner frowned. 'Appleby – do you know? I've a vague notion this may be your fourth hoax. Shall we find out?' The Commissioner's hand hovered over a switch on his desk. Then he glanced at his watch. 'Or shall *you* find out? A great shame, your dropping in only at such short notice. Got to lunch with the Minister, the Lord help me.'

'And I've wasted too much of your morning already. Turn me on to one of your chaps.'

'Yes, I will. Damned nuisance, working lunches. Barbarous phrase, barbarous idea, eh?'

'I'll do a working lunch on my own – at my club and with the Braunkopf file. If, that's to say –'

'My dear chap!' The Commissioner was delighted, and he now flicked a switch enthusiastically. 'We've been losing ground steadily since you insisted on having your cards,' he said humorously. 'In all except the most trivial technical ways. The Braunkopf file can be located and photo-copied for you in three minutes flat.'

'I'm most grateful.' Appleby picked up his hat – the bowler hat which it amused his family to remark he kept for expeditions to Town. 'And perhaps I'll go along to the Da Vinci as well.'

'Never been there,' the Commissioner said, and chuckled. 'The voonderble vorlt has never been my line.'

Chapter Four

At one of the small tables by a window – where nobody could do more than pause beside you for a moment and exchange a few words – Appleby ate steak-and-kidney pie and washed it down with a frugal third of a bottle of claret. Every now and then he resisted the solicitations of a large and enthusiastic waitress who was convinced that he would be better for a little more boiled cabbage. Clubs – or at least this club – had taken to some oddly changed ways. But through the window the spectacle and the muted sounds were unchanged: a glint of steel, a clatter of hoofs as a troop of Horse Guards clattered down the Mall. Appleby, however, was not occupied with the view. The sheaf of papers he had brought away from Scotland Yard absorbed him – so much so, that he almost allowed the exuberant waitress to follow up the steak-and-kidney pie with a dollop of apple-dumpling. Just in time, he raised an arresting hand, and switched the gesture to point at the passing Stilton. Then he returned to his reading.

It was certainly in the character of an aggrieved citizen that Mr Braunkopf – with a noble scorn for any merely local police force – had presented himself at Scotland Yard. He had once, it appeared, sold a colour lithograph to the wife of the Home Secretary; and he had thus been in a position to represent himself as the acknowledged prime purveyor of aesthetic delectation to the entire Cabinet – a body of men (and ladies) notably distinguished for their connoisseurship and artistic taste. Thus representing himself, Mr Braunkopf had been received with the immediate respect such connections command in a democratic society. He had, it was true, been a little demoted later; but by that time he had established himself in the regard of several senior officers entirely on his own merit. It could not be claimed for him that he owned any notable brilliance of mind, or even much that was positively inspiring in point of moral posture. But in the middle of much dreary routine, Mr

Braunkopf could undeniably be quite a success for half an hour.

He had been the victim, it seemed, of an outrageous imposture. And it had been shrewdly, he was constrained to admit, that he had been singled out as victim. Only a man who habitually took an elevated view of human nature, who expected fair and honourable dealing in return for fair and honourable dealing, could have been so shamefully betrayed as he had been.

Mr Braunkopf, it appeared, had been approached by the confidential agent of a nobleman in relation to an artistic problem of some delicacy. Beguiling a dreary winter day by rummaging through some ancestral lumber, this nobleman had come upon a darkened canvas of the most evident antiquity, curiously concealed (as it seemed) beneath a tumble of mouldering folio volumes chiefly of a theological nature. So much was the subject of this painting obscured by heavy varnish, that the nobleman had not at first accorded it much attention. Suddenly, however, he had seemed to distinguish one *motif* – and then, while in the very act of blaming the impurity of his own mind for having imagined something, he had undeniably distinguished another. It was a highly indecent picture.

The first impulse of the discoverer of this opprobrious object was, of course, to occasion its immediate destruction. But he then reflected that he was not, perhaps, entitled to do this; that here, conceivably, was something which would prove of interest to art historians. It might even be valuable. So he had made discreet inquiries, and followed these up by taking equally discreet measures to have the canvas cleaned. What emerged in consequence surprised him very much. It appeared that a certain Giulio Romano (of whom he had never heard, but who turned out to be the only painter to have achieved the distinction of being mentioned by William Shakespeare) had enjoyed considerable esteem in the earlier sixteenth century. In fact he had been nothing less than head of the Roman school of painting in succession to Raphael, and most of his work had been of an edifying, not to say a sacred, character. He had done an important 'Benefactors of the Church' and an even more important 'Donation of Rome to the Pope'. Unfortunately he had fallen into the reprehensible habit of devoting some of his leisure hours to compositions of a different character. Most of these were mere drawings – notably a set to accompany certain licentious sonnets composed by Pietro Aretino. (The nobleman had been able to turn up Aretino in his own library, translated into very comprehensible French.) But once, at least, Giulio had done an oil painting in the same manner. It was known as 'Nanna and Pippa', and had been very celebrated in its time. Several detailed descriptions of it were extant. Long ago, however, it had disappeared, and historians were inclined to suppose that, after agreeably adorning for many years one of the more private apartments of an art-loving cardinal, it had been destroyed by a succeeding cardinal during a fit of religious morbidity. But this could not in fact have been so. For here the 'Nanna and Pippa' was – discovered under the collected works of Bishop Stillingfleet in the possession of an English peer.

The confidential person who had consulted Mr Braunkopf explained the resulting situation frankly. His principal (whose anonymity must be maintained) was not minded to expose such a work to the curiosity of his family and guests either in his town residence or in his country seat. He had made tentative moves to present it to the National Gallery, but it seemed that there would be a similar difficulty in placing it on public exhibition there; only properly accredited scholars could be exposed to the risk of corruption and depravity inherent in contemplating this creation of the Roman *caposcuola* in so decidedly off a moment. So what was to be done?

It had occurred to the nobleman that there were private collectors – notably, perhaps, in the United States of America – whose catholicity of taste would incline them to treat Nanna and Pippa (who were clearly delightful girls) as they deserved. And who might pay to be allowed to do so. But such a negotiation required a high degree of discretion as well as wide experience in such matters – the more particularly since, the quieter the deal, the more convenient might it be in point of certain financial dispositions purely private to the painting's present proprietor. Hence the recourse to Mr Braunkopf.

Mr Braunkopf had highly commended to the confidential person his sagacity in coming straight to the Da Vinci Gallery. It was a concern, Mr Braunkopf had modestly pointed out, of the very highest reputation and the most unblemished ethical standing in the entire voonderble vorlt. Mr Braunkopf then proposed (after having received satisfactory assurances about percentages and the like) that he should proceed at once to the nobleman's residence for the purpose of examining Giulio's painting. But this had proved unacceptable. The nobleman was minded that – for the time being, at least – his identity should remain unknown even to the eminent dealer whom he had caused to be sought out. The Giulio, however, would be brought to the Da Vinci on any date that should suit Mr Braunkopf's convenience. And Mr Braunkopf could there arrange for its due authentication by the very best authority on Mannerism (Giulio being undoubtedly the founder of that interesting school) available in England.

This had come about. The painting had appeared; eminent authority had appeared; eminent authority (after due admonishment as to the highly confidential character of the whole affair) had made its expertise, pocketed its fee, and departed. And then the still unknown nobleman's agent (who had brought the canvas in under his arm) raised a further interesting point. The nobleman, it appeared, had by this time become rather fond of Nanna and Pippa. He liked, it might be said, the way they comported themselves. So he proposed having his discovery copied before parting with it. In a purely private apartment (the nobleman's bathroom, the confidential person confided to Mr Braunkopf with the ghost of a conspiratorial smile) he judged that a modest replica would look uncommonly well. For this purpose the painting must be removed again for a brief space. But within a week it would be back in Mr Braunkopf's keeping.

This too had come about – or had appeared to. And when the confidential person reappeared with the painting he had a most interesting communication to make. The state of his principal's affairs was such, he now confided to Mr Braunkopf, that very considerable expedition was to be desired in the further stages of the operation. The nobleman – not to put too fine a point on it – was damned hard up. Mr Braunkopf was distressed by this news. Being (as he explained to a senior and poker-faced Inspector at Scotland Yard) one eminently well affected to the Crown and Constitution of these islands, it harrowed him to hear of any vulgar pecuniary embarrassment befalling an ornament of the

Sovereign's Court. So distressed was he, that he had an immediate suggestion to make. He was prepared to enter the affair no longer as an agent but as a principal. He was prepared to make an immediate offer for the Giulio himself. Whereupon the confidential person, while expressing proper astonishment and gratification at this outstanding posture of magnanimity on Mr Braunkopf's part, did confess that his client had borne some such possibility in mind – and that as a consequence he, the confidential person, was empowered to close the deal there and then, cash down. And Mr Braunkopf would understand that by cash what was meant was *cash*. The agreed price would do in ten-pound notes. But five-pound notes would be even better.

Mr Braunkopf was, of course, well accustomed to transactions in which the peculiar needs of the other party – often, he believed, the greater ease which such a system afforded to the unobtrusive handing over of substantial sums to charity – entailed dispositions of this kind. After what might be called a decent ritual haggle, he repaired together with the confidential person to his bank in the next street, withdrew the required sum in notes, handed it over there and then, and returned to the Da Vinci Gallery with a comfortable sense of the day's work well done. He was not at all sure of what he might eventually obtain for an obscene painting – untraced through nearly four hundred years – by Giulio Romano. It might not prove to be astronomical, but it would certainly very much exceed the mere £12,000 which he had just parted with. So after putting in a quiet half-hour selling another colour lithograph (eighteen guineas, plus five guineas for mount and frame), he repaired to his inner sanctum to refresh himself with the contemplation of his new acquisition. It was remarkable, he thought, how perfectly the pigments had been preserved beneath their now departed layers of varnish. It was very remarkable, indeed.... Mr Braunkopf (who was a frank and unaffected man) admitted to the Inspector that his first realization of the truth had actually been occasioned by hearing himself give a howl of rage. The higher connoisseurship, after all, is a highly intuitive affair. At one moment Mr Braunkopf had been modestly pleased with himself; in the very next moment he *knew*; a moment after that again, he had turned the picture round, and was looking at the back of a perfectly fresh and innocent canvas on its stretcher. It wasn't even a forgery that had passed into his possession. It was an honest-to-God copy of an original which – he instantly realized – he had seen once but might never see again.

There were several more pages of the Braunkopf file. But, having read so far, Appleby knew that he had in effect read all. Criminal Investigation would prove to have shed no light on this ingenious fraud. He flicked back a page, and glanced again at the name of the man who had authenticated the picture. It was an odd fact about expertises that the eminent scholars qualified to make them made substantial fees at the same time. Indeed, it was a unique fact. Among top archaeologists, for example, anything of the kind wasn't on; they grumbled about it, but were rather pleased with themselves all the same. So with the picture boys, you had to know your man. Appleby knew this man by repute; he was a respectable professor at Cambridge. Which meant that the Giulio Romano he inspected had been a real Giulio Romano. Or at least that was a good working hypothesis. Somewhere in the world (barring the intrusion of another cardinal in a morbid frame of mind) the thing existed still: Nanna and Pippa, two high-class tarts, done in oils by a painter who hadn't, in fact, been too good with oils, but who was an extremely important figure in the history of Western art, all the same. This canvas, unknown for centuries, had suddenly turned up at the Da Vinci Gallery, transported thither by a person unknown and from a place unknown. Perhaps it had simply been whisked away briefly from an unsuspecting owner: the evident train of events required no more than that – an hour or two for the Da Vinci and the painfully hoodwinked Braunkopf; perhaps no more than two or three days for the attentions of an expert copyist. Alternatively, the owner of the Giulio had hit upon the bright idea of selling his painting twice over: once to Braunkopf and once to somebody else.

But consider – Appleby said to himself – the context in which this deception appears to place itself. Lord Cockayne and the predatory August Personage. Sir Thomas Carrington and his Stubbs. The worthy Mr Meatyard and his visit to Sir Joshua Reynolds. It was a reasonable hypothesis that these three had been defrauded by a single far from unmercenary joker, thoroughly well up in the craft of peddling pictures. If this were so, then it was a fair bet that the business of the Giulio Romano tied in and followed the same pattern. Once more, that was to say, there had been a carefully planned operation against an ingeniously chosen victim. The 'Nanna and Pippa' was really extant; there could be no doubt of that. But as its whereabouts had been unknown, it must be supposed that its owner, somewhat oppressed by its dubious character, had kept entirely quiet about it. He had probably felt himself to be in the position of a gentleman who keeps a collection of erotic books in a cupboard. As a consequence, he had been in no hurry to make a fuss when something a little irregular had occurred. Yes – Appleby told himself – that might well be it. The Giulio had vanished from its discreet niche, but with some intimation that it had merely been borrowed – as a joke, it might be represented – and would be returned quite soon. Absolute theft might have nerved the owner to call in the police. But the appearance of a mere prank would make him hesitate – and then (the painting having been authenticated at the Da Vinci and copied meantime) back it had actually come. So the only substantially aggrieved person had been Braunkopf, and Braunkopf had no information which would provide the police with any sort of trail.

So here, once more, was the formula: lucrative fraud perpetrated in such circumstances that ridicule or a fear of ridicule acted at least as an inhibiting force – as a kind of brake, one might say – upon the vigour and effectiveness of any come-back by the defrauded person.

Having arrived thus far in reckless speculation, Appleby pulled himself to a halt. You really had to be a very retired policeman indeed, he told himself, thus cheerfully to run ahead of the evidence. Of the four undoubtedly curious affairs he had been reviewing he was equally without any first-hand information – without the slightest brush or contact with any of the personages concerned. One was no more than a yarn spun to him by a young man in an Oxford college. Two were memories of matters once brought to the police but very little pursued – and certainly never before directly inquired into by Appleby himself. The fourth was in more or less the same category as the second and third, but had been after his time. There had, indeed, been more rigorous investigation on this occasion, Braunkopf having alleged so large a loss. But nothing seemed to have come of it. Braunkopf himself apart, there seemed to be no witness to tackle. Except, indeed, Professor Sansbury of Cambridge, who had set eyes not only upon the authentic 'Nanna and Pippa' but also, presumably, upon the mysterious confidential person who had produced it. As for tangible evidence – anything of the order that, in court, could be termed an exhibit – there was the copy of 'Nanna and Pippa'. (At least it might be supposed there was that, still in the possession of Braunkopf.) And that was the lot. There didn't seem much scope for manoeuvre.

Appleby tucked the Braunkopf papers back in their file, and glanced round the dining room. The average age of those lunching (he had calculated on a previous occasion) was about five years short of the age at which those male persons die whose age at death is recorded by their sorrowing relatives in *The Times* newspaper. In the year 1968, that was to say, here was a roomful of people who were quite strictly to be defined as Victorians. But – Appleby had turned his head a little further – there was one surprising exception. Quite a young man had strayed into the club. He could conceivably have done so, of course, only as a guest – and indeed there was a more than reasonably elderly man at the same table with him. They were father and son, or uncle and son, or conceivably grandfather and son. And about the young man there was something familiar.

It was no doubt only because his mind had been far away that Appleby was thus for a moment tardy in recognizing so recent an acquaintance as Lord Oswyn Lyward. For it was certainly he. Here, rather oddly, and dutifully sipping port in evident deference to his host, was the prime mover of Appleby in his present courses. Nor could there now be much doubt as to who was entertaining him. Father and son had been the correct conjecture. Here was Lord Cockayne himself.

The young man glanced up, and caught Appleby's glance. On his part, recognition was immediate. He jumped to his feet, and strode across the room.

'Oh, I say, sir!' he said. 'What luck running into you in this mausoleum. Won't you come over and meet my father?'

Chapter Five

Lord Cockayne stood up – an action which the difficulty of the operation rendered all the more gracious in this amiable nobleman. For Lord Cockayne was distinctly ancient; surprisingly so, indeed, for the father of an undergraduate son. Within his tweeds – which had once been of a peculiarly hairy variety, but were now worn smooth except in quite small patches – he creaked alarmingly as he moved. This was the more disconcerting in that, for the moment at least, Lord Cockayne appeared tolerably well oiled. He had lunched comfortably and was now taking no more than a second glass of port, but perhaps he was to be accounted among that class of elderly persons whose heads lighten as they age. It was with a certain vagueness of direction that he extended his hand.

'How-d'y-do?' Lord Cockayne said. 'Glass of port?'

Appleby agreed to a glass of port. He couldn't recall having seen Cockayne in the club before, and he wondered whether he often favoured it with his presence. This speculation received, as it happened, an answer now.

'Like to give Oswyn lunch here once in a way,' Lord Cockayne said. 'Good atmosphere, eh? Self-made fellows with plenty of effort in their lives: bishops, professors, top sawbones, smart chaps at the Bar. The boy should take their measure, you know. See what he's up against. As my father used to say to my brothers: younger sons must be prepared to take their place in the ranks.'

'Has Oswyn chosen a particular rank yet?'

'I'm working on it all the time.' Lord Oswyn Lyward gave Appleby the ghost of a vulgar wink. 'I have serious thoughts of the Foreign Service. Hard work, of course. But great scope.'

'New fangled name for the thing,' Cockayne said. 'But goes on much as before. Boy might do worse.' He watched Appleby take a first sip from his glass. 'Unassuming stuff, eh? But port is in a confused way, these days – very confused, indeed. Shocking situation at Keynes, I may say. '55 is thought to be pretty good, though, and should start its drinking life soon. Before I end *mine*, I hope.' Lord Cockayne acknowledged his own witticism with an appreciative bark. 'And now about this picture.'

'Yes, of course.' Appleby betrayed no astonishment at this abrupt intimation that he had been summoned into Cockayne's presence for professional purposes. It must be Oswyn's doing. The young man had clearly taken it into his head that there was amusement to be extracted from stirring up this ancient matter.

'Sorry your son's not lunching with you,' Cockayne said – much as if it had occurred to him that his preparatory civilities had been inadequate. 'Bobby, eh? Been down to us once or twice. Brains. Straight bat as well, I'd say. Good stable-companion for Oswyn here. Always delighted to see him. Regret we haven't met his mother. My wife knew her family very well.'

Even as something thus announced politicly in a past tense, this was news to Appleby. He murmured suitably.

'My father thinks,' Oswyn prompted, 'that we should have that picture back.'

'Quite right,' Cockayne nodded approval. 'Joke's gone on long enough. Happened some years back.'

'That puts it mildly,' Appleby said. 'Wasn't Lord Oswyn still in his pram?' He paused on this question – which appeared, however, to produce only perplexity in Lord Oswyn's father. There was more conducing to the old gentleman's vagueness, one had to conclude, than a mere injudicious matutinal recourse to port. His wits were far from what they had once been. Appleby wasn't sure that this rendered altogether agreeable his son Oswyn's resolve to extract diversion from planting that ancient hoax or fraud once more actively on the carpet. On the other hand Appleby – although the Lywards, father and son, couldn't be aware of it – was in London precisely for the purpose of poking into the series of mysteries which seemed to begin with their affair. So he couldn't very well do other than go along with them now.

'Fact is,' Lord Cockayne was saying, 'that somebody may have got away with something valuable. Been suggested to me before, you know. Was even suggested to me at the time. Perhaps something in it, eh? Value of things changing. Old Canadine – nice chap I met for the first time lately – telling me the other day of a thing he'd have called a garden ornament. His father – the Canadine there was the scandal about, you know, when some actress poisoned herself – had shoved a pipe through it and made a damned indecent sort of fountain of it. Pissing into a little pool, Appleby, not to put too fine a point on it. All right with statues of small boys, I suppose. Kind of thing the Italians call potties.'

'*Putti*,' Oswyn said.

'But this wasn't a small boy. Well, one night the thing simply vanished from the middle of its pool. At first Canadine thought very little about it. No great opinion of his father's taste, I suppose – and, anyway, he thought what the thieves had been after was merely the value of the lead running through the thing. Its urinary system, one might say.' Lord Cockayne suddenly looked surprisingly hard at Appleby, as if his reception of this harmless joke was to be a test of him as adequately a *sahib*. 'But then some guest or other, who'd seen the statue before and turned out to be a bit of a connoisseur, told Canadine it was probably quite devilishly old – Graeco-Roman, as the art-wallahs say – and probably worth a tidy sum. You see what I mean?'

'I think I do.' Appleby had put down his glass, and was staring at Cockayne. 'And would I be right in supposing that the present Lord Canadine was rather reluctant to make a fuss?'

'Quite right. Or rather, he had been, at the time the statue was made off with. He'd just made a speech in the Lords, as it happened, about pornography and so on. You know the kind of thing. *Lady Chatterley's Mother*.'

'*Lover*,' Oswyn said.

'Exactly, my dear boy. So it would have been rather embarrassing to call in the coppers. But when he was tipped the wink that this Venus, or Diana, or whoever she was, might be valuable –'

'He regretted his delicacy of feeling.' Appleby didn't venture to glance at Oswyn, who was clearly deriving keen satisfaction from this colloquy between his elderly companions.

'Just that, Appleby. And I'm dashed if I don't feel rather the same about my picture. Of course, one wants to do the decent thing by these people –'

'Of course,' Appleby agreed gravely. It was obviously the Royal Family who were being thus described.

'But there are limits, after all. If this dashed daub was by Duccio –'

'Or Pollaiuolo,' Oswyn said, 'or Mariotto Albertinelli, or Pietro Berretini da Cortona.'

'Any of those.' It was not without suspicion that Lord Cockayne glanced at his youngest son. 'It would be a different matter, eh? I certainly think we should have the thing back. And let the long-haired chaps have a look at it.' Lord Cockayne finished his third glass of port and looked quickly at Appleby. 'How long will it take?' he asked briskly.

'To recover your painting? Not, I hope, as long a time as it has been lost for. But you must consider that, if it is really valuable and was stolen because it was designed to make money out of it, then it probably passed through various hands long ago.'

'Very true, of course.' Cockayne nodded with a great appearance of sagacity. 'But you must come down and have a look round on the spot. Finger-prints and so forth, eh? Get that boy of yours to bring you. He knows our ways.'

Appleby, although doubtless gratified at having thus attributed to his son a familiar acquaintance with aristocratic courses, produced only a cautious reply. Only the day before, he had been announcing to Judith a positive determination to penetrate to Keynes Court. But now, as his old professional instinct was rekindled in the face of this whole bizarre affair, he had an impulse to preserve for himself a complete freedom of action. Moreover the notion of the slightly dotty Lord Cockayne breathing down his neck while he pottered round Keynes Court looking for finger-prints carelessly disposed there a generation ago was ludicrous rather than appealing. Moreover, just at the moment, he had a strong sense that Mr Hildebert Braunkopf of the Da Vinci Gallery was his immediate quarry. It was true that the anti-pornographic Lord Canadine, so awkwardly circumstanced because of his father's indelicate comportment with a Graeco-Roman antique, constituted another beckoning presence. His small misfortune certainly belonged with the series, and enforced the conclusion that somebody variously well versed in artistic matters had been master-minding the whole thing. But Appleby didn't know Lord Canadine, and he did know Mr Braunkopf. There had been a time when he was almost an authority on the workings of Mr Braunkopf's mind.

So Appleby got up with appropriate murmurs, and took his leave of the Lywards.

Something had happened to the Da Vinci Gallery since his last visit. On that occasion Mr Braunkopf had assembled a number of works by Pietro Torrigiano – a surprising number, considering the known paucity of anything portable by that celebrated contriver of monumental sculpture. But then Mr Braunkopf was an enterprising man. In the modest window of his establishment, Appleby recalled, there had been exhibited a large photograph of the head of Joseph of Arimathaea from Michelangelo's celebrated *Pietà* in Florence. It is well known that this is a self-portrait of Michelangelo – which is why Joseph is represented with a broken nose. For Michelangelo had his nose broken as a boy and by another boy, when the two ought to have been engaged decorously in the study of Masaccio's frescoes in the Brancacci chapel. This second boy – three years younger, indeed, than Michelangelo – was none other than Torrigiano, whom it has in consequence been incumbent upon all good Florentines to hate ever since. These interesting biographical particulars, appearing in neat print beneath St Joseph and repeated in the catalogue which Mr Braunkopf had prepared for his patrons within, had somehow had the effect of authenticating the objects on view. So (for the guileless, at least) had the scrupulosity with which a few bore descriptions like 'Possibly an *atelier* piece' and 'Thought by Prof. Salignac to be by a pupil during the Seville period' and 'Almost certainly a copy by Gerard Christmas (ob. 1634)'. A congruous background, moreover, had been provided for the battered memorials of Torrigiano's industry. The eroded stones and the shards of painted terracotta had been niched and nested protectively in sombre velvets, and the few bronzes were lit by very subdued spotlights. Mr Braunkopf had been subdued too; he had put aside the more exuberant of his *persona* (the Duveen one) in favour of the muted and hieratic stance which his intimates understood to be modelled upon the late Mr Berenson.

But today all this had vanished. The not very extensive façade of the Da Vinci had been given a coat of brilliant acrylic paint; and in the interior, too, it might be said that everything had changed utterly, and a terrible beauty been born. The window, indeed, prepared one. Gone were the compassionate, if broken-nosed, features of St Joseph, and in their place hung what appeared to be an enormous blow-up from a strip cartoon. The face of a lady done in dots or stipples each the size of a six-pence was pensively posed upon an elongated and obtrusively manicured hand; and lest one should miss the implication of this brooding guise there was a wavy line ascending from the crown of her head to a bubble in which was inscribed the single word *THINKS*. Appleby (being a trained detective) had no difficulty in interpreting this evidence. Mr Braunkopf and the Da Vinci (for a few weeks, at least) had gone Pop.

And Mr Braunkopf himself was on view. This, indeed, was the only way in which he could with propriety be described, so triumphantly had he achieved the appearance of being – so to speak – one of his own exhibits. Gone was the Duveen outfit which had been so finely congruous with Pietro Torrigiano, and which had been closely modelled upon the more formal morning attire of King George the Fifth. Instead of Savile Row Mr Braunkopf had betaken himself (it was to be supposed) to the neighbourhood of Carnaby Street. Except for his years (and, even more, for his figure, which was yet more rotund than of old), Mr Braunkopf was indistinguishable from one of those almost young gentlemen who alternate minstrelsy for the million with the final summits and acclivities of mystical experience. His nether limbs were encased in brilliant orange jeans so constricting as to suggest that they had been assembled on his person by a particularly muscular tailor required in some surgical interest to provide him with a new and permanent outer integument. Above this, Mr Braunkopf ballooned out in an ample velvet garment, predominantly magenta in colour, but with anything that might have been overpowering in this tastefully relieved with silver braid and unexpected excrescences in fur and feathers. On a slender chain round Mr Braunkopf's far from slender neck hung a small silver bell.

Becoming aware of Appleby, Mr Braunkopf rang the little bell with vigour. He then advanced with arms raised in a gesture combining astonishment, welcome, and a hint of priestly benediction.

'The goot Sir John!' Mr Braunkopf said. 'Vot happinesses – yes, no? You come in the van?'

'I've simply walked –'

'And my other goot freund patron Lady Abbleby parking her limousine, puttikler difficult this distrik now on account of all these nobles gentry and other carriage persons' – Mr Braunkopf gestured confidently at his largely untenanted rooms – 'eagersomely frequenting this prestigious manifestation the Da Vinci Gallery?'

'My dear Braunkopf – I don't, to begin with, keep a van in London, and –'

'You come in the van, yes, and Lady Abbleby in the rearguard, no?'

'Oh, I see. No, my wife is in the country. She'll be sorry to have missed your show.' Thus masking his evil intentions from the innocent Braunkopf, Appleby glanced round the exhibition. It ran, he saw, to Op as well as Pop. There were some three-dimensional contraptions so delicately exploiting the principle of parallax that they appeared to be in ceaseless movement merely because it is impossible to maintain the organs of human vision perfectly immobile in space. Others, of grosser motion, required to be plugged into the Da Vinci's electricity supply; they were a kind of aesthetic sophistication, Appleby reflected, of those coin-operated automata which had rendered glamorous the railway-platforms and seaside piers of his childhood; one or two were constructed, by a perverse ingenuity, out of cheap plastic materials which would have contrived to be sensuously repellent even in the mere unworked sheet or slab. Most of the pictures on the walls operated – rather more successfully – on similar lines. The spectator was looking at a wilderness of hypertrophied advertisements and strip-cartoons, and in doing so he was also looking at designs of great formal precision and purity. Appleby found these disguisings and collidings disconcerting.

They also made him aware of his umbrella and bowler hat. And Mr Braunkopf – a perceptive man in certain limited professional relations – appeared to read the signs and act on them.

'For you and me, Sir John, it is not so goot, no? Our vorlt is vorlt of puttikler prestigious Old Masters Mantegna Martini Masaccio Masolino Magnasco Michelangelo Michelozzo, yes?' Having thus – and as it were by means of some interior consultation of a Dictionary of Art – achieved this roll-call of the great, Mr Braunkopf paused impressively. He seemed to have forgotten the surprisingly trendy character of his present attire. 'But for the yunk, Sir John, there is differences. For the yunk all this ephemerious art' – Mr Braunkopf's gesture round his gallery was now indulgent and patronizing – 'is inciting, yes? Say for the enthusiastical but incriminating children of my goot freunds Sir John and Lady Abbleby. I keep one two three four special pieces this inciting art for birthday presents the incriminating children my goot freunds. Not expensive. Quite some not so expensive as the yunk would guess.' Mr Braunkopf lingered appealingly on this last consideration. It was a favourite with him when the purchase of a present appeared to be in prospect. 'You buy, Sir John, leaving me choose special bargains account our long cordial dissociation?'

'Well, no, Braunkopf. I'm afraid not. Nothing quite of that sort today. I'm looking for something rather different, as a matter of fact.' Appleby contrived to glance round about him in a cautious and even furtive fashion. 'I have an uncle, you see, who is a very old man, and uncommonly rich. Fond of pictures, as it happens, and I thought it might be nice to make him a little present.' Appleby lowered his voice significantly. 'But what he likes are – well, pictures of a certain character. You understand?'

It was evident that Mr Braunkopf understood. Nor did he betray any sign of finding at all out of the way the appearance in the Da Vinci Gallery on such an errand of a retired Commissioner of Police. Dignified and unperturbed deliberation was what his attitude now suggested. His establishment was known, after all, to be an almost preternaturally ethical concern. Its monolithic character in this regard was no doubt such that it could suffer a chip or two from time to time without much noticing.

'A goot class of *erotica*, yes?' he murmured. 'Sir John, you please stamp this way. You stamp into my sanctum quick look three four superior *curiosa*-type vorks of art for authentink connoisseurs. Henry Fuseli, Sir John. Most respectful reputacious artist and religious person. Royal Academician, the same as John Constable, Thomas Gainsborough, J. M. W. Turner.'

'I don't think my uncle would care to own any Fuselis. As you say, Fuseli was a clergyman before he turned artist. That would make my uncle a little uneasy, I feel. As a matter of fact, I have something else in mind. An old colleague has told me about the shameful manner in which you were deceived about a Giulio Romano. I gathered you suffered a heavy financial loss.'

'That was nothings, Sir John.' Mr Braunkopf produced a lavishly careless gesture which failed entirely to obscure the sudden wary expression on his face. 'A large concernment like the Da Vinci, with close connectings Paris New York San Francisco Berlin Milan Valparaiso, is undefected by such small swindlings. Sir John, I have one puttikler genuine ancient Roman brothel scene –'

'What has struck me, Braunkopf, is that you must still possess the copy of the Giulio that you were left with. A firm of your reputation couldn't think of putting such a thing on the market. I suppose you have it simply stowed away somewhere on the premises?'

'Of course, Sir John. Entiresomely of course.' Mr Braunkopf – Appleby felt himself instructed to observe – was now almost agitated. 'But, Sir John, I have two three voonderble stimulacious top-class pornographical –'

'I'd like to see the copy of the Giulio now, please. As a matter of fact, Braunkopf, I might take it off your hands at a moderate price. If Nanna and Pippa are what they are cracked up to be, you know, my uncle would probably like them very much. And he wouldn't care a damn about the thing being a copy. So a deal might be to our common advantage, wouldn't you say?'

Braunkopf had palpably no inclination to say anything of the sort. He was looking at his good friend Sir John Appleby with something like animosity. Appleby naturally found this interesting. It had been quite on the spur of the moment that he had invented a salacious uncle for himself. Now he had a sudden suspicion that this freakish performance was going to pay off; that revelation, if only of a minor order, was just round the corner. And this persuasion increased with him at Braunkopf's next move.

'Misfortunately, Sir John, it is not possibles.' The harassed proprietor of the Da Vinci spread out apologetic hands. 'I just recollek this small trifling fraud been loaned to manifestation of fakes frauds forgeries copies National Museum of Patagonia.'

'I think we'll find it has come back.' Appleby spoke gently but firmly. He knew where he stood with Hildebert Braunkopf. It was one of the many points of good citizenship in that estimable man that he had a wholesome respect for the police. 'In your strong-room, I suppose it will be?'

And Mr Braunkopf, having hesitated for a moment, emitted a fat and dispirited sigh. Then, with a beckoning motion, he waddled slowly across his gallery. It was almost with compunction that Appleby followed him.

Nanna and Pippa were undoubtedly nice girls. Unfortunately they were represented as occupied in a fashion that could not possibly conduce to edification. It was evident that Mr Braunkopf felt this keenly. However laudable was his good friend's desire to give pleasure to an ageing uncle, it was painful to see one of Sir John's scrupulous refinement actually brought into the presence of this lascivious spectacle. It was not even as if it were the authentic work of Giulio Romano, and therefore contemplatable in the saving consciousness that it was worth a lot of money. So anxious was Mr Braunkopf to obviate the flaw in taste and decorum which had produced this confrontation that he even – after a two-minute session with the canvas – suggested to Appleby immediate adjournment to another room in order to enjoy the modest pleasure of a glass of champagne.

It had taken Appleby less than these two minutes, however, to realize that he was now experiencing – as it were in reverse – what had befallen Braunkopf on the occasion of his agonizing discovery. Braunkopf had thought to see an original painting and become aware that he was seeing a copy. Appleby had thought to see a copy and was suddenly convinced that he was seeing an original.

'I'll give you two hundred guineas for it,' he said.

'But, goot Sir John, it is not the reasonables!' It was patent that Mr Braunkopf's agony was extreme.

'Come, come, Braunkopf. Except as a curiosity, the thing has no value at all. One can have pretty well any picture in the National Gallery copied for fifty pounds. To refuse four times that amount for this is very odd indeed.'

'It has what we call the association interest, Sir John. An unfortunate episode in the history of the Da Vinci. I should have the unhappiness in parting from it.'

'You mean you have a sentimental regard for it? But of course you don't.' Appleby took three brisk steps forward, and suddenly reversed the painting on the easel upon which Braunkopf had reluctantly placed it. What was revealed was the back of a very ancient canvas indeed. 'My dear Braunkopf, you really weren't careful enough. You took it into your head that you had been cheated into accepting a copy. But it was the real thing, safely back again. And here it is.'

There was a moment's silence, while the unfortunate Braunkopf digested these ironical observations. Then, if he did not positively rise to the occasion, he at least accommodated himself to it.

'Sir John,' he said with dignity, 'I must make you the confidences.'

Chapter Six

'It was authentink criminous fraud,' Braunkopf presently resumed. He had had the hardihood to withdraw from his sanctum for a couple of minutes, and return with two glasses and a half-bottle of champagne. Appleby, who was able to tell himself that he was in no sense a police officer on duty, accepted this refreshment without demur. The ritual production of wine and cigars upon important occasions was one of the proprieties of Braunkopf's world, and there would be no advantage in turning it down. And Braunkopf, thus indulged, solemnly raised his glass. 'Sir John,' he said, 'it is hip-hip hurrah three cheers, yes?'

'Well, yes – although I believe that, as a toast, it is commonly contracted to "cheers". Cheers, Braunkopf.' Appleby let some moments decently pass before adding firmly: 'You are asserting that the story you told at Scotland Yard was true?'

'But of courses, Sir John!' Always a man of delicate feeling, Braunkopf had plainly struggled not to let too much of surprise and reproach sound in this response. 'Only I did not quite give credences that this low immoral picture was truly in the possession of anonymous nobility gentry like for instance my goot freunds Sir John and Lady Abbleby the Duke of Horton the Duke of Nesfield K.G. other my goot freunds patrons the artisocracy. It would be aspersious – yes? – to suppose any members the British artisocracy have dealings feelthy peectures.'

'Your sentiments do you great honour. What you are saying is that you didn't believe this story of a nobleman discovering a Giulio Romano by accident among a lot of lumber?'

'That is so, my goot Sir John. One develops the instinctuals, no? I had the instinctual this Nanna and Pippa belong some low-born wealthy person collector feelthy peectures now weeding out some few paintings perhaps buy others feelthier.'

'It sounds a more likely story, I agree. But I'm surprised it didn't make you a bit more wary. For you were caught out in the end, weren't you? Despite this being here now' – and Appleby pointed to the authentic Nanna and Pippa on their easel – 'you *were* landed with a copy?'

'Yes, Sir John. Just how I told the police, all authentink and above plank.'

'But you didn't remain altogether above board with them for long? You cooled off in your real wish to assist them, I think? And it was because you had yourself thought up something better?'

'That is correck, Sir John.' Braunkopf seemed not at all perturbed by these somewhat hostile questions. 'I put on my thinking hat. And soon I stopped believing anybody had made proposings to themselves to sell this puttikler shocking picture at all.'

'Ah!' Appleby was now really interested. 'You conjectured that it had simply been abstracted from the possession of its owner – conceivably without that owner's knowledge – and brought to you, along with a plausible story, for the purpose of that expertise by Professor Sansbury, as I think it was?'

'Correck, Sir John.'

'It would then have been copied – again on the plausible story presented to you – before being restored to its normal location. And the copy was brought back to you – with the result that you were caught off your guard, and persuaded to part with a great deal of money for it?'

'Twelve thousand pount, Sir John!' There was the liveliest pathos in Braunkopf's voice as he recalled this sum; he seemed quite to have forgotten that it was a mere trifle in the regard of such a solid institution as the Da Vinci Gallery.

'Well, something has happened since then.' Appleby again glanced at the authentic Nanna and Pippa. 'I think you had better tell me just what.'

'I was determined on destitution.'

'That does seem one way of looking at it. You'd been uncommonly careless, if you ask me.'

'It would only be justice, no?' Braunkopf showed himself as

having been perplexed by Appleby's last remark. 'I had a right to destitution.'

'Oh, I see. You certainly had a right to restitution, if the criminals and the cash they had made off with could be traced. But it isn't the cash you've ended up with. It's the picture. Go on.' Appleby paused invitingly. But Mr Braunkopf, although not to be described as normally an unready man, was reluctant to proceed. He replenished Appleby's glass. He walked over to the easel, contemplated Nanna and Pippa fixedly, and contorted his features into what was evidently designed as an expression of deep moral reprobation. 'Did you trace it and steal it?' Appleby asked.

'My goot Sir John!' Braunkopf was even more shocked by this than by the flagitious spectacle on the canvas before him. 'I recovered this piece my own property only by most puttikler ethical derangement.'

'I'm not clear that it ever was your own property. You can't make a valid purchase, you know, of something the other fellow doesn't possess the right to sell. And it can't be said you made much inquiry into the matter when it first came your way. But that's by the by. I shall be most interested to hear about your ethical arrangement. Am I right in thinking that you began by consulting whatever knowledge you have of known collectors of blue pictures in this country?'

'Exakly, Sir John. As Proprietor and Director this notable Da Vinci Gallery I make a puttikler study business deficiency. We file purchasers clients other goot freunds according to known special and particulous interests in whole voonderble vorlt of art.' Mr Braunkopf, as he touched this cherished and sublime expression, looked regretfully at the empty half-bottle on his desk; he had erred in hospitality (he must have been feeling) in treating so particularly good a friend as Sir John Appleby to so meagre a symposium. 'And natchly, Sir John, there is a blue file. There has to be a blue file, Sir John.' Mr Braunkopf paused for a moment, as if dimly feeling that this contention ought to be substantiated. 'All the colours in the spectrum – no? – must go to the composings the glorious sunlightings that voonderble vorlt. So I vork through them all.'

'All the collectors of dirty pictures?'

'High class, only.' Mr Braunkopf sounded his reproachful note. 'Nothink to do with pornography, no? Pornography is for middle-class persons; nobles gentry and all stimultaneous Da Vinci clients have refined interest in *erotica*.'

'I think we can cut out all that.' It certainly seemed to Appleby that it would be fruitless to pursue Braunkopf's singularly confused morality and sociology. 'You drew up a short list, I imagine, of persons whose tastes in this direction were backed by fairly substantial means. It was a most rational proceeding. But how did you subsequently contrive contacting them?'

'Bargains, Sir John.' Braunkopf beamed at the innocence of the question that had been directed at him. 'I take a portfolio with some six ten top-class drawings regrettables. And I offer these regrettables at low figure suitable persons. Then I achieve conversion.'

'I rather doubt that.'

'I achieve conversion on various art topics. Relaxed conversion, Sir John, puttikler appropriate between established collector and reputacious dealer. Then I lead the conversion round to security, a most puttikler important topic collectors of regrettables. On account insurance, Sir John. One regrettable in a collection of respectables is easy to insure. But too many not, yes?'

'So I should imagine. So you got these people to discuss security, and thefts, and so forth. No doubt you represented yourself as having connections which might make you more effective in recovering pictures, were a robbery ever to occur, than are the police. And credit where credit is due, Braunkopf. You'd make a very good job of that sort of talk.'

'My goot Sir John, that is great kindnesses in you.' Braunkopf seemed genuinely moved by the tribute thus paid to him. 'And so, you see, I come to the owner this high-class regrettable.' He gave Nanna and Pippa a wave. 'It was my goot patron Mr Praxiteles. My *late* goot patron Mr Praxiteles.'

'I find it hard to believe in the existence of a man with such a name. And do you mean he's dead?'

'Mr Praxiteles, Sir John, is a most wealthy and high reputacious ship-owner. And not defunk. Not that at all.' Somewhat surprisingly, the ghost of a grin hovered on the dignified features of Mr Braunkopf. 'Just no lonker a goot patron the Da Vinci Gallery.'

'I see.' Appleby glanced rather grimly at the Da Vinci's proprietor. 'This fellow Praxiteles was the owner of the Giulio Romano, and he was foolish enough to disclose the fact to you – with the further information that it had been stolen, or at least made away with for a time?'

'Exackly, Sir John. Removed from his collection by unknown depradatious persons, who left a note that only some jokings was intended, and that soon the Nanna and Pippa turn up again.'

'It has already struck me that that might be the way of it. So your precious Mr Polyclitus –'

'Praxiteles, Sir John.'

'Praxiteles decided to keep mum for a little, and just hope the picture *would* come back, rather than risk embarrassing publicity? Then, sure enough, his faith in human nature was rewarded, and back it did come.'

'After I had bought it, my goot Sir John.' Braunkopf made this point urgently.

'Not exactly that, as a matter of fact. When the authentic picture came to you here, you were proposing to act merely as an agent. You bought the copy – and no doubt after the original had been returned to Praxiteles. And now we come to the final act in your disreputable comedy, Braunkopf. You got the original out of Praxiteles, and here it is. Are you prepared to tell me just what persuasion you used? Not, I imagine, another cheque for £12,000.'

'No, my goot Sir John, not that.' Braunkopf produced this in a judicial tone, as if here had been one of the courses of action which he had envisaged, but which he had turned down for another equally reasonable. 'Not exackly that.'

'Not that at all, I rather suspect.'

'Sir John, I was entirely fred.'

'You were entirely what?'

'I was entirely fred and open with Mr Praxiteles. I spilled him the whole peas.' Braunkopf made a virtuous gesture. 'Nothink was concealed from him, account high ethical standing the Da Vinci Gallery.'

'In particular, I think, you didn't conceal from him that

57

you had placed the matter of the fraudulent sale of the copy to you in the hands of the police?'

'Correk.'

'And that you would now have to tell the police of Praxiteles's ownership of the original?'

'Natchly, Sir John. A citizen must give the police all assistings –'

'Quite so. But you didn't fail to point out to this reputable ship-owner that the result would be a great deal of embarrassing publicity?'

'It was not the necessities, Sir John. Mr Praxiteles is most intellectuous smart person.'

'I don't doubt it. And you proposed a deal to him. He was to let you have the original, and you would let him have the copy?'

'Correk. Praxiteles is not a true lover, Sir John, of the voonderble –'

'He just liked Nanna and Pippa, and was prepared to put up with the copy, and let you blackmail him –'

'My goot Sir John!'

'And let you blackmail him out of a good many thousands of pounds' worth of property, for the sake of preventing this rediculous and unsavoury business from being made public. You were on pretty strong ground with him, I can see. But at least you've lost a customer.' Appleby paused briefly, and then pointed to Giulio's picture. 'Why is it still here? Why haven't you sold it by this time to some other Mr Praxiteles?'

'It was the destitution that was important, no? Now I have the destitution, and there is no need to be precipitatious. The market for regrettables is very delicate one, Sir John – puttikler for high-class ethical concern. This prestigious *chef-d'œuvre* Giulio Romano problesome shipped to United States of America.'

'I see. Nanna and Pippa are waiting to be rolled up and sent across the Atlantic inside the exhaust-pipe of a car?' Appleby looked again at the painting. 'Or perhaps you'll get some poor devil of an art-student to overpaint it with an English rural scene – in stuff that will come away again under a sponge?'

'Not a rural scene, my goot Sir John.' Braunkopf was suddenly indulgent before this inexpertness. 'It is necessitous to

58

follow the main lines of the existential composition, yes?' He paused meditatively. 'Perhaps a "Christ in the House of Mary and Martha", no?'

'I don't think I need trouble you further at the moment. Except with a small piece of advice.'

'Yes, my goot Sir John?' Braunkopf – an intelligent man, who knew when he was in a spot – spoke with a resigned meekness.

'No Mary and Martha at the moment. And no anything else. Put this thing back in your strong-room and leave it there. I can make no promises. But the extent to which my heart bleeds for Mr Praxiteles is a very moderate one. Not, you know, that it bleeds any more for you. And now, good afternoon to you. And thank you for the champagne.'

'It is always the privileges, Sir John.' Mr Braunkopf was all esteem, and indeed affection. 'You will make my complimentings to my goot freund and patron Lady Abbleby, yes?'

'I suppose so, Braunkopf.' It was not the first time that Appleby had felt defeated by the resilience of the proprietor of the Da Vinci Gallery. 'In fact, yes – I will.'

'And to my equal goot freunds the yunk Abblebys, yes? Reminding them this present prestigious manifestation strikly contemporary art at most modersome prices –'

Appleby picked up his hat – his London bowler hat – and fled.

Chapter Seven

Walking back to his club through the filtered London sunshine, Appleby reviewed his accumulated material. There was rather a lot of it – almost what might be called an *embarras de richesse*. Five distinct frauds had swum within his ken.

Lord Cockayne had been robbed of a small picture by an unknown hand. It might have been entirely valueless. But if this fraud was in fact connected with the others, then the general pattern suggested that it was something worth a lot of money. How could the thief have known this? Here was a first question to which there was no answer at present.

Sir Thomas Carrington had almost certainly been the fortunate owner of an authentic specimen of equine portraiture by George Stubbs. Since Stubbs had happened to paint horses, dogs, curricles, phaetons, barouches, chaises, and the like, whether with or without their squirearchal owners and their wives, with an exquisiteness never achieved by any other painter, Sir Thomas must be supposed to have suffered a very considerable monetary loss indeed.

Mr Meatyard, affably conducted by Sir Joshua Reynolds round his studio, had been sold, so to speak, a pictorial pup. What it had cost him was unknown, but had certainly been as much as a cleverly calculating rogue had thought it useful to ask.

Lord Cockayne's noble friend Lord Canadine had been the victim of the simplest of these stratagems. He had merely suffered the theft of what he regarded as a garden ornament, but which in fact might be vulgarly described as in a different price-bracket altogether.

And Mr Praxiteles – with whom the series closed at present – had been deprived for a brief space of a work of art by Giulio Romano: this in order that Mr Braunkopf might be defrauded of £12,000. Mr Braunkopf had then, in effect, defrauded Mr

Praxiteles of a like sum. So Mr Praxiteles, and not the designed victim Mr Braunkopf, had here eventually ended up as the loser.

So much – Appleby thought, as he began to walk down Lower Regent Street – for the skeleton of the affair. But that it was an 'affair' at all – that one aspect of it really did cohere with another – depended upon one's accepting the significance of certain common features. The most striking was the exploitation, by the villain or villains concerned, of what had to be termed the embarrassment factor. Lord Cockayne had been told, by a posthaste emissary from an exalted quarter, that there would be discomposure and distress in that same quarter if he didn't keep mum – and being by tradition and training a proconsul of Empire he had at once toed the line. There had been clever calculation behind that. Sir Thomas Carrington had merely wished not to look awkward as having offered to the Royal Academy (or whatever the body was) a Stubbs that perhaps had never been a Stubbs at all; and this had been enough to make him pull his punches. Mr Meatyard, at first noisily indignant, had seen himself heading for a figure of fun. Lord Canadine had been in the habit (one had to suppose) of leading his male guests (no doubt on a late-evening stroll in summer) to view, in some secluded corner of his demesne, a joke not readily to be accommodated with a refined modern taste. Mr Praxiteles had been similarly circumstanced; he would not be eager to publicize his possession of a choice collection of curious pictures; this had kept him mum when his – possibly temporary – loss had been discovered, and had subsequently made him knuckle under to the resourceful Braunkopf as well.

Most of this, Appleby told himself, he had totted up already. But there were two further points of significance. The first was the highly specialized character of the operations. Somebody had *known* about Lord Cockayne's unsuspected treasure, had *known* that Sir Thomas Carrington possessed a Stubbs, had *known* not only that Lord Canadine's garden ornament dated from classical antiquity but also that it had been treated in a disrespectful manner, had *known* about the sort of pictures collected by Mr Praxiteles. It was only the misfortune of Mr Meatyard that was a little out of series here, but it still fell within the general area of operations in the art-market. And the second point was at least a related one. The entire sequence of frauds, although seemingly yielding big money every time, was too freakish to be thought of in terms of a professional criminal world. When that world impinged upon the art-world – upon Braunkopf's voonderble vorlt, one might say – it was usually by way of stealing masterpieces and holding them for a ransom which insurance companies or wealthy owners were often willing to pay up in an unobtrusive way. In operations of that kind there was really big money – money comparable with what might be gained by robbing mail trains and bullion merchants – and with this the gains from these bizarre operations, substantial though they must have been, simply didn't compare. The whole lot, in fact, had something amateurish about them. But amateurish in the old-fashioned sense of the word. The element of fun or play – or of practical joke, if one cared to put it that way – distinguishably lurked in them.

But then again – and Appleby paused on the steps of his club – the mind behind them was quite as wary as it was crazy. It was a mind capable of biding its time, and of so minimizing risks. The series of five frauds covered a period, according to his reckoning, of over fifteen years. The perpetrator, that was to say, was capable of lurking and watching for two or three years before finding conditions which sufficiently assured him of success.

Was there anything else to be remarked of these outlandish *coups* collectively? Appleby suddenly saw that there was. He himself had much the same attitude to all of them, and it was an attitude which could best be described as distinctly lacking in moral zeal. He had retired from keeping a professional eye on crime; he had no more than the private citizen's obligation to resist it; and in the matter of these odd goings-on he had been inquiring into he found that he had no serious feelings at all. If Oswyn Lyward was reliable – which was perhaps a large assumption – his father had lost nothing he had valued; and between Mr Braunkopf and Mr Praxiteles as deserving or undeserving characters there was clearly nothing to choose. And so on, indeed, through the whole lot. This surely meant that he had come up to town in a thoroughly idle spirit. He might as well have stayed at home, and filled in his time with a chess problem or a crossword puzzle.

Appleby found this sudden glimpse of himself as a busybody discouraging. Lord Cockayne appeared really to want him to go down to Keynes Court, but this was upon the strength of expectations so unrealistic as not in fact to constitute a very sensible proposal at all. He had been able to impose himself upon Braunkopf, and extract a certain amount of hard information from him, largely because of that wary gentleman's politic insistence that in Appleby he had the good fortune to be firmly possessed of a powerful friend and patron. When Braunkopf got round to divulging dubious practices to you – and Appleby had experienced this with him before – it was almost impossible to resist the premise that the matter belonged with what Braunkopf liked to call the confidentials. At Scotland Yard Appleby's successor had been entirely amiable, but he had probably regarded his visitor as having turned harmlessly eccentric all the same. How would Lord Canadine regard him – or Sir Thomas Carrington or Mr Praxiteles or Mr Meatyard – if he simply presented himself with a ring at a front-door bell?

Appleby nodded abstractedly to a porter, hung up his hat and umbrella, wandered into a smoking-room, decided it wasn't too early to ask for a drink, and sat down with an evening paper.

'You can't maintain we're too bad at prediction,' the Astronomer Royal was saying. 'It's our speciality, in a way. I can predict you a very nice line in comets, for instance, pretty well stretching out to the crack of doom. There will be an effluxion of just so much time –'

'Whatever *that* may be,' the Astronomer Royal's companion said.

'Ah, yes – of course. Time. Yes, indeed. One has to make use of these rather vague terms. But so much of what we call time will go by, and there will be your comet, as punctual as a tube train drawing up at a platform. If it's a day or two late, the world's astronomers will be thrilled to bits.'

'Yes, yes – predictability, of course.' The Astronomer Royal's companion, whom Appleby didn't know, was looking at the Astronomer Royal with a great appearance of severity. 'I ought to have said repeatability. Repeatability is the test, wouldn't you say?'

'Certainly, my dear fellow, certainly. But it depends so much, you know, on one's lab. And on the extent to which one can potter around one's lab. Mine is fairly commodious – nothing less then the spacious firmament on high – and I can claim to be coming to wander around it fairly freely. And I don't mean in their ridiculous hardware. Like every competent astronomer, I am steadily extending my own means of strolling through interstellar space. But strictly as a looker-on. I'm rather like Appleby here. Do you two know each other, by the way? Sir John Appleby, Professor Sansbury. For Appleby, crime is now among what may be termed the spectator sports. But whereas he has simply become a touch-line character on retiring, I am essentially one while still more or less actively on the job. It isn't even any good my giving an encouraging cheer. The stars in their courses heed me not. So I can't get them to square up in the interest of the repeatability principle.'

Apart from a conventional murmur at the appropriate moment, Appleby had said nothing. It struck him as odd – as conceivably, indeed, an instance of what is termed the finger of Providence – that here, fortuitously before him, was the eminent Cambridge art historian who had authenticated the Nanna and Pippa. But he was even more impressed – or depressed – by the Astronomer Royal's having so firmly characterized him as a mere *spectator ab extra* in the murky firmament of crime. It was perfectly true, and just what he had been thinking himself. Like the astro-physicist, he was without power to give anything a nudge or shove as it went by. But *was* this quite true? As he asked himself the question, Appleby was aware of a new glimmer on the farthest fringe of his mind. If he wasn't exactly like Keats's watcher of the skies when a new planet swims into his ken, he was at least a man in whose mind a little astronomical talk had lodged a new idea.

'Repeatability?' he now asked. 'You're talking about the principle of the controlled experiment?'

'Something like that.' The Astronomer Royal passed a hand over his abundant silver hair. 'Have you ever interested yourself in psychical research – parapsychology, as they say nowadays?'

'I read about it from time to time.'

'At Cambridge,' Professor Sansbury said, 'it has been admitted within the sphere of orthodox scientific inquiry. For that matter, eminent scientists have been interested in it for a long time. But now there is a new statistical basis. Most interesting.'

'My point is, you see, that these fellows are in rather the same position as myself in point of this repeatability business. We both have to bide our time. Take the affair they call ESP. Turning over a set of cards, you know, and having somebody guessing about them in the next room. The experiment isn't, in the strict sense, repeatable – simply because this paranormal faculty comes and goes in such individuals as seem to be endowed with it, and sometimes there seems not to be anybody available at all. You can think up new techniques for investigating the phenomenon, and have no end of stuff ready waiting in your lab. Gadgets for recording and measuring electrical behaviour in the brain, and so forth. And then you just have to *wait* – you see? – until some sort of suitable percipient turns up. It's rather the same with astronomers. We have everything ready and waiting – and then what used to be called the celestial objects take their time in coming along.'

'But at least they come along predictably,' Sansbury said. 'Whereas these extra-sensory people mayn't come along at all.'

'Quite true – but they can keep us waiting the devil of a long time. I sometimes do wish I could lure or summon the stars out of their courses.'

'Lure them?' Appleby said.

'Have everything set up for them and waiting, you know. And then drop them a line, saying we'd prepared the ideal little theatre for them to show their paces in. A straight appeal to astral vanity, as it were.'

'Most interesting.' Appleby seemed quite impressed by these whimsical remarks. 'There's an astronomer in Dr Johnson's *Rasselas* –'

'My dear Appleby, I read about him every year on my birthday. A cautionary tale for us, indeed. "I have sometimes turned aside the axis of the earth, and sometimes varied the ecliptick of the sun." I could quote you the whole thing. The poor old chap hadn't been content simply to admit himself a looker-on, and as a result the stars drove him off his rocker. Sansbury, are there any professional risks of that sort in your line?' The Astronomer

Royal glanced at his watch as he spoke, and jumped to his feet. 'Only don't give me the answer now, or I'll miss my damned train. Time, once more. Good day to you both.' And he turned and strode from the room.

'A fanciful mind,' Sansbury murmured. 'But entertaining enough for a short time. And I suppose the answer to his question to be that, in my line, we run small risk of going mad, but a considerable risk of making asses of ourselves.' He paused, and glanced at Appleby curiously. 'Do you often drop in here?'

'Not nowadays. I live in the country, and seldom come up to town. Today I've been looking up a few old acquaintances – including one whom I think you know. Hildebert Braunkopf.'

'Braunkopf?' For a moment the name seemed to convey nothing to Sansbury. And then he nodded. 'But, Lord, yes! Fellow who has a picture-shop he calls the Da Vinci? I once thought I'd made an ass of myself *there*, as a matter of fact.'

'Over a couple of tarts?'

'Tarts?' Not unnaturally, Professor Sansbury was startled. But then he laughed. 'By Jove, yes! Nanna and Pippa. You know something about that affair?'

'I may almost be said to be investigating it.' Appleby announced this boldly. Indeed, he now knew in his heart that he *was* investigating it. For hadn't an altogether surprising idea come into his head? 'You see,' he went on to Professor Sansbury, 'I happen to have made contact with a rather similar case. It happened in the household of a friend of my youngest son's. Keynes Court – Lord Cockayne's place.'

'How very interesting.' Sansbury – who had given Appleby a sudden sharp glance – sounded suitably impressed. 'You mean another business of a picture's being borrowed, authenticated, copied, and returned? That was the species of foolery I was involved in through this Da Vinci concern.'

'No, not quite that. Just straight theft.'

'I see. But round about the same time as this Giulio Romano affair?'

'Well, no. The Keynes Court incident was over fifteen years ago.'

'Dear me.' No doubt justifiably, Professor Sansbury stared at Appleby.

'I assure you there are some grounds for tracing a connection between the two events.'

'And with other events as well – perhaps within this fifteen years period?'

'Well, yes.' It was Appleby's turn to stare. Sansbury appeared to be a more astute character than he had supposed. 'But it is Braunkopf's misfortune that I want to start off from. You don't mind my discussing it with you for a few minutes? This chance meeting is quite a stroke of luck for me.'

'My dear Sir John, I don't object in the least. I'd be delighted to think the affair was going to be cleared up. It gave me at least a bad half-hour.'

'When you heard Braunkopf was asserting that what he'd been finally landed with was a copy?'

'Precisely so. Of course I was quite clear that what I had been asked to go and look at in the first instance was an old painting. Indeed, I hadn't the slightest doubt that it was Giulio Romano's Nanna and Pippa, of which there is a good deal of early documentation. But when I did hear Braunkopf's news, I naturally wondered at first whether I could have been taken in by a clever forgery. Fortunately, as soon as I saw the thing –'

'You did see the copy, as well as the original?'

'Naturally. The police were investigating the matter, and I was asked to go along to this Da Vinci place again. Fortunately – as I was saying – there was no question of the canvas being the one I had previously seen and authenticated. It was a perfectly straight, and very recent, copy. I'm surprised it took the fellow Braunkopf in, even for a quarter of an hour. He simply can't have examined his purchase properly before paying up. But then the whole trick was cunningly contrived to take him off his guard. And so, I suspect, was the whole cock-and-bull story that was pitched at him.'

'Why do you suppose it to have been that, Professor?'

'My dear sir!' Sansbury appeared to be almost at a loss before this question. 'It was a story about a nobleman finding this picture in a lumber-room. That's a hoary old yarn in itself. And when it proves to be the prelude to an unscrupulous fraud, it would be absurd to accept it for a moment.'

'Then what do you take to have been the true background of the affair?'

'I can only say that several perfectly good guesses are possible. It is simplest to suppose that the deception upon Braunkopf was perpetrated by the present owner of the picture. He exposed it to expertise, deftly took it away again, returned a mere copy, and nevertheless collected a large sum of money. He has the money in his pocket, and the original picture available for surreptitious sale elsewhere. It's that kind of picture, after all. But there's another possibility – and it's the one I've been accepting. The rightful owner of the thing may be totally innocent. It may have been briefly borrowed without his knowledge.'

'Quite so.' Appleby was undecided for a moment about how much to divulge. Then he decided to take this eminent figure in the world of connoisseurship at least partly into his confidence. 'But the truth, as a matter of fact, appears to be a little different from either of these assumptions. The picture was stolen – or, rather, it was borrowed for the purpose of the fraud. The owner was aware it had gone, but he kept quiet about it. He had been given some assurance that it had been taken as a mere prank, and would be returned to him. And so it was.'

'Its character made him reluctant to create a fuss?'

'Yes. Which reminds me, Professor, of that bad half-hour. Was it partly a matter of the character of the thing with *you*?'

'Well, yes –·I suppose that's a fair way to put it.' Sansbury laughed not altogether happily. 'Of course, indecent pictures exist, and one can hardly decline to make one the subject of an expertise. But I certainly didn't relish such a thing making the headlines. I couldn't have looked other than slightly ridiculous. Fortunately it never attained to the dimensions of a sensation. I have a notion that Braunkopf himself began to drag his feet in the affair. Perhaps he felt the reputation of his wretched little gallery –'

'Perhaps. Or perhaps he found his own way of getting square on the deal.' Again Appleby hesitated. 'I agree that it isn't a particularly pleasing picture to become associated with.'

'You've seen the copy? Braunkopf has hung on to it?'

'I've seen the original.'

'The original! You're sure?' This time Sansbury was really startled – perhaps almost alarmed. 'The true owner is known to you?'

'It depends on what you mean by the true owner, Professor. I have reason to suppose that the identity of the man who *was* the true owner is known to me. But my sight of the authentic Nanna and Pippa has been in Braunkopf's shop. He at least regards himself as the true owner now. He says it has come to him by way of restitution.'

'Restitution! What the devil does he mean?'

'He was £12,000 out of pocket on account of the authentic picture, and so has felt himself entitled to get hold of it. It's as simple as that.'

'You mean that the disreputable creature has stolen the thing? Surely the police –'

'Braunkopf hasn't exactly stolen it. He has simply persuaded the owner to exchange it for the copy – pointing out to him that it is not socially salubrious to become widely known as the possessor of a whole cabinet of indecent paintings and the like.'

'It's absolutely incredible!'

'Not really. Braunkopf, although caught napping when he handed over all that money, is far from being a stupid man. And he has really taken a leaf out of the other fellow's book. The owner kept quiet once – when the thing was borrowed, that is – because he didn't want publicity. So Braunkopf saw that there was a chance he would allow himself to be imposed upon again. After all, the fellow still has a representation of two courtesans curiously employed, and that's what he chiefly cares about.'

'There's something thoroughly nasty about this, I must say.' Professor Sansbury had pulled out a pipe – presumably by way of indicating that he was by no means impatient to get away. 'I begin to see, Sir John, that you are pretty heavily involved in this matter in a professional way, and perhaps I ought to leave asking questions to you. But I must say I'm curious about the identity of the chap who has this collection of curious pictures. Is it indiscreet to ask his name?'

'He's a Mr Praxiteles. Braunkopf says he's a ship-owner.'

'Never heard of him.' Sansbury sounded almost regretful. 'I suppose you're going to chase him up?'

'I'm not exactly entitled to do that. But I think it quite likely that I shall take means to make his acquaintance. Meanwhile, Professor, would you mind if I asked you about just one point?'

'Fire away.' Sansbury had now lit his pipe. 'The honest truth is, you know, that this is beginning to interest me very much.'

The smoking-room had emptied itself. There wasn't even so much as an old gentleman asleep in a corner of it. Only an ancient club servant was going round, emptying ash-trays, straightening chairs and folding newspapers. After dinner a few members would drift in again. But in the main people dined for the purpose of playing bridge afterwards – and that transacted itself in a sepulchral chamber upstairs. One could have continued here in almost perfect privacy till midnight and beyond, discussing the most intimate affairs.

'What I'd like to go back to,' Appleby said, 'is the original cock-and-bull story. The nobleman with a lumber-room is said to have started out with a laudable desire to present Nanna and Pippa to the nation. Then – rather inconsequentially – he thought of finding an American buyer through the instrumentality of Braunkopf. But he was determined to remain entirely anonymous –'

'It really was the most awful bosh.'

'I rather agree, and we needn't suppose that Braunkopf swallowed quite all of it. But what interests me is the supposed intermediary. The confidential person, I mean, who was supposed to be contacting Braunkopf on the noble person's behalf. It occurs to me that you must have encountered him.'

'Of course I did. He brought the picture to Braunkopf's place, and remained brooding over it while I examined it. But it must have been after I left that he told Braunkopf the story about the owner wanting to have it back for a few days in order to have it copied.'

'Just how did this expertise work? It seems that you satisfied yourself on the spot. I'd have imagined that perhaps laboratory tests might have been required.'

'There might have been something in that.' Sansbury now spoke indulgently. 'Raking light, and so on, might have revealed characteristics of the *fattura* – the handling, you know – not perceptible to the naked eye and relevant to whether Giulio Romano painted the thing. But nothing of that sort was my business. I looked at it – and just that, you will understand, is my job – and wrote and signed an opinion that it was the original Nanna and Pippa. I suppose I spent about twenty minutes on the commission. Feeling a bit of a fool, as a matter of fact.'

'Again because of the subject matter?'

'Well, yes. An elderly man, peeking and peering at what is going on in the damned thing. You must understand that the particular handwriting of the painter in representing some quite small detail of a figure or gesture –'

'I can see that you might feel the situation to be a shade absurd. But I don't suppose Braunkopf did?'

'Not in the least. He made quite a solemnity of it. Do you know? It seems to me that the perpetrator of the fraud was rather skilful in inventing a nobleman as the picture's owner. Braunkopf seemed decidedly to "dig" the nobility, as the young people might put it.'

'He had a good deal to say about nobles gentry his goot freunds?'

'Just that. But I expect the fellow you're particularly interested in is the intermediary.'

'Decidedly so, and I wish I could see him at all clearly. You had no feeling, I suppose, that you'd ever seen him before?'

'Absolutely not.'

'And you haven't set eyes on him since?'

'I'm quite sure I haven't.'

'It would be too much to hope for, I suppose.' Appleby paused for consideration. 'As I've hinted to you, Professor Sansbury, I am interesting myself in a group or sequence, spread over a considerable period of time, of affairs roughly in the same general area as this one.'

'You whet my curiosity very much, Sir John. Not that I have any business to be curious.'

'I shall be delighted to tell you more about it, some time when you are at leisure.' Appleby presented this civil evasion promptly. If anything more was to be done today, he had not a great deal of leisure himself. 'A few of these frauds and impostures must have required something like a gang to carry them out. But it strikes me that the one we are considering could have been a one-man show. We know that this chap who brought the picture to the Da Vinci was not really acting as the agent of a nobleman – nor of any other rightful owner of the thing. So was he any sort of mere emissary or confederate at all? May he not have contrived the entire imposture on his own?'

'Even to the extent of subsequently painting the copy, Sir John? He'd have to be uncommonly versatile. Burglary on the one hand – for I suppose that's how he did his borrowing – and highly competent painting on the other. And he'd have had to know about this person Praxiteles and his collection.'

'The man I'm looking for knows his way around such matters very well indeed. By the way, would you call the man we're talking about young or old?'

'Between young and youngish. Probably not much more than thirty. Which would rule him out, as far as Keynes Court goes.'

'Perfectly true.' Appleby again reflected that Professor Sansbury was one whom not much got by. 'If I really am in contact with a single group of frauds, it isn't your Da Vinci friend who has master-minded the lot. Did he strike you as potentially a master-mind?'

'I can't think any such idea came into my head.' Sansbury was amused. 'As far as I can remember, he said very little.'

'Should you recognize him again?'

'Oh, yes – I imagine so. Unless he were in some way disguised.'

'Should you recognize his mere voice?'

'That's rather more difficult to say. But probably not.'

'There was nothing peculiar or characteristic about it?'

'Nothing at all. It was an ordinary upper-class English voice.'

'That sounds rather important to me, Professor. In fact, he was a gentleman?'

'He wasn't anxious to suggest the air of one.' Sansbury was speaking with care. 'Now that you mention it, I was struck by that at the time. But it's hard to express. It was rather as if he was playing a part. A little too many "Sirs" in his talk, and that sort of thing. Wanted to suggest himself as out of a lower social drawer than in fact he was. Funny how sensitive we English are to all that.'

'No doubt. But we seem to have arrived at something, even if it's nothing much. This fellow was performing a mere henchman's role, and it didn't come quite naturally to him. And we may suppose that the head of the gang – if there is a gang – had nobody more verisimilar to assign the job to.'

'It reminds me of books I used to read as a boy.' Sansbury's amusement had grown. 'Crooks who were at the same time great social swells. Somebody-or-other the Amateur Something.'

'Raffles, Professor. And Cracksman.'

Chapter Eight

Left to himself, Appleby let his mind continue to dwell for a few minutes on Nanna and Pippa, or rather on the problem of which they were the centre. He knew more about this affair than about any of the others, but he still didn't know very much. It was clearly desirable that he should meet Mr Praxiteles, now the owner of these ladies only in what might be termed the shadow of a shadow. For an erotic painting, one had to assume, must be rather a frustrating object in itself. A mere replica of it must appear yet more remote from the real thing.

Mr Praxiteles might not be easy to meet. Appleby had a notion that persons of his kidney put in a good deal of their time cruising in the Mediterranean on board rather notably well-appointed private yachts. No doubt they kept an eye on their mercantile interests that way.

On the other hand Mr Praxiteles, if encountered, might be persuaded to converse. There was something about that quite small fragment of his history now known to Appleby which suggested that his fibre might not be all that tough. He seemed not to have put up much of a show against the unblushing blackmail of Hildebert Braunkopf. For Braunkopf had got away with exactly that. He had threatened Praxiteles with highly inconvenient publicity if he refused to exchange an extremely valuable object for a worthless one. Braunkopf must have known that Praxiteles could be intimidated.

But meeting Mr Praxiteles – even if he were on *terra firma* and in England – required a little thinking out. Appleby had no standing in his affair whatever. It was only with Lord Cockayne that he had anything of the kind. Or rather – he was visited by a sudden thought – with Lord Cockayne by invitation, and with Sir Thomas Carrington (the Stubbs man) and Mr Meatyard (the Sir Joshua Reynolds man) by a species of indirect association. When their misfortunes had come the way of Scotland Yard Appleby had, after all, been running the place. He hadn't, of course, himself seen either of the defrauded gentlemen, or taken any part in investigating their not very pertinaciously preferred complaints. But at least he had heard about them. Some capital could be made out of that.

Appleby looked at his watch. At a pinch they could not merely find him a room in the club but produce the customary adjuncts of civilized slumber as well. And he could simply ring through to Judith. But first he had better check on whether anything could in fact be done that evening. Carrington was almost certainly a totally rural character, coming up to town once a year for a house dinner or the Eton and Harrow Match. Meatyard, on the other hand, sounded a metropolitan type. He would live surprisingly close to the West End in a surprisingly suburban sort of villa of the more commodious – or indeed imposing – type. Appleby made his way to the telephone directories. There wouldn't be all that number of Meatyards in London. It was the sort of surname a lawyer would strongly advise you against dropping into a novel or a play.

But what *was* a meatyard? Flicking through the pages, Appleby found time to ask himself this question. Had he ever found himself in a meatyard? No. Had he ever heard such a place mentioned? No. It was probably fallacious to equate Mr Meatyard with, say, Mr Cowmeadow or Mr Swineherd. 'Meatyard' was a corruption of something highly Anglo-Norman. This Mr Meatyard (the Sir Joshua one) was not in fact a simple citizen who had been practised upon as a consequence of defective education. He was simple because effete. He would prove to be like Lord Cockayne, only very much more so.

Appleby found his man, and dialled his number.

'I went into it,' Mr Meatyard said. 'I went into it thoroughly. I couldn't have Reynolds. So I saw to it I had *him*.'

'It's a superb portrait,' Appleby said – and reflected that it was a good beginning not to have to tell a fib. The picture dominating the lounge – it was certainly a lounge, for the vision of Mr Meatyard as of Norman blood had not fulfilled itself – was of a comfortable lady in middle life. She was distinguishably dressed for her occasion, but was not in the least swayed by any uneasy consciousness of the fact. She had sat to the greatest of living European painters, and been entirely equal to it.

'I owed it to Martha,' Mr Meatyard said, with quiet satisfaction. 'I'd been had for a proper Charlie – eh, Sir John? But give me time, and I do find my way about.' Mr Meatyard pointed firmly at the portrait of Mrs Meatyard. 'Would you exchange that for one of their Reynoldses? Just answer me straight.'

'I can't be certain that I should.' Appleby smiled. 'Is that straight enough?'

'I'll make do with it.' Mr Meatyard (who, oddly enough, turned out to deal in meat in a very big way) gave Appleby a shrewd look. One wouldn't have supposed Mr Meatyard at all easily taken in – but then even very capable men can be curiously at a loss in fields remote from their own. 'I looked into Reynolds, you know. I followed him up at that place down on the Embankment – the one named after the fellow who made money in sugar. Lyle, is it?'

'Tate.'

'That's right – Tate. Well, I looked at Reynolds there, and in a good many other places as well. It seemed to me he painted invalids mostly. Nasty green tinge in their complexions, wouldn't you say? I don't think I'd care to have Martha looking like that.'

'You felt you were well clear of Reynolds?'

'Now you're having your laugh at me, Sir John. And plenty of other people, back when this happened, looked like having their laugh too. I didn't like the idea, I don't mind telling you. Still, I look back to it now in what you might call a kindly way. It's brought me a lot of pleasure, and that's a fact.'

'Being fooled, Mr Meatyard?'

'No, no. This business of painting and painters. I'd never given it much thought before – although, mark you, we had all the proper things in the house. Everything hand-done – except for etchings and the like, which are no more, you might say, than half-and-half. But then I took to this looking into it – starting with your Reynolds, who I tell you I don't think much of. But do you know Gainsborough, now? Lived at very much the same time, it seems. I took to Gainsborough. I've got a couple by him in the next room. Then Cézanne.'

'Cézanne?'

'Not in Gainsborough's class, of course, since he comes in a hundred years later. Pricey, all the same. I wouldn't like to tell you what I had to pay for my Cézanne. I just wouldn't have signed the cheque, Sir John, except for the feeling he gives me. As if I was inside that canvas, and moving around. You know what I mean? I've worked it out it has something to do with how all those flat slabby bits lean this way and that. Orderly, too. Like good book-keeping, you might say. A pleasure to look at.' Mr Meatyard paused. 'Yes,' he said contentedly. 'I find I'm very fond of pictures. Would you ever have been in Florence, by any chance?'

'Florence?' Appleby contrived to be perfectly solemn. 'Yes, I have been there.'

'There's a very good golf-course.'

'A golf-course?' This time, Appleby was pretty well caught off his guard. 'What an extraordinary thing!'

'Very creditable it is, considering the climate. But I just don't take my clubs there now. Too many pictures. Martha and I go round and round the Uffizi. A nice place. Clean toilets, and a very tolerable snack to be had, looking down over the city. But the pictures are the thing. Painted to absolutely top specifications, and more of them than you'd believe.'

'They are certainly very notable.' Appleby found he was failing to take a proper pleasure in this unexpected sequel to Mr Meatyard's encounter with the spurious Sir Joshua. That his mild misadventure should have brought into the worthy man's life hitherto unknown satisfactions in the field of aesthetic experience was no doubt a wholly gratifying circumstance. But it didn't look like being of much use to Appleby in his self-imposed quest. A more forthright approach seemed required. 'At least,' Appleby went on, 'you've got wise to a good deal by now. You wouldn't be taken in after the same fashion again.'

'I'd like them to have another go at me, Sir John. I'd show them a thing or two, mark my words.'

'I'm afraid they're not likely to single out the same victim twice. But they are in business still – or that's my guess. And it's why I've called on you. You must admit that, once you'd recovered from your first annoyance at being defrauded by this bogus Sir Joshua –'

'It wasn't so much that. It was their making a fool of Martha, you know. That, and disappointing her so. Ringing the bell at this great painter's studio, and nobody there. That was what took me to the police.'

'The impulse did you credit, Mr Meatyard. But then you backed out. Wouldn't that be a fair way of putting it? I ask because I can see that you're a fair-minded man.'

'Well, in a manner of speaking, yes. I saw that we'd have all the papers laughing at us. Martha wouldn't have liked that.'

'So you minimized the whole affair by naming a totally inaccurate sum as what you'd been cheated of.'

'And just how would you substantiate that, Sir John?'

'My dear sir, it is quite self-evident. An elaborate imposture of that sort isn't mounted for the sake of peanuts.'

'Well, now, Sir John – that would depend, wouldn't it? An imposture may be a fraud, or it may be a hoax. And doesn't this sound more like a hoax – a practical joke – than a fraud? Here is a self-made man – Albert Meatyard, with no education to speak of – believing that he can have Mrs Meatyard's portrait painted by Sir Joshua Reynolds. It's a regular scream, wouldn't you say? And if they top off their bit of fun by getting twenty pounds out of him for some worthless painting, that's as great a lark as if they got twenty thousand. And is modest enough to keep them out of gaol, likely enough, if they're found out. The fellow on the bench – one of your public school and 'varsity men – is amused by the whole thing.'

'I see all that. In fact, I keep on seeing something very like it in connection with one or two other affairs. But be honest, Mr Meatyard. You were had for a proper Charlie – and in solid L.S.D.'

'£8,000, Sir John.' Mr Meatyard – whom Appleby was beginning to take to – suddenly smiled cheerfully. 'A stiff bill for the start of an education in art, you might say. And I'll show you what I got for it. Painted by hand, sure enough. But you couldn't say much more than that.'

'£8,000?' There was the most innocent surprise in Appleby's voice. 'Not peanuts, of course. But not far off it. You have been a minor victim, Mr Meatyard.'

'A *minor* victim?' Perhaps for the first time, Mr Meatyard glanced at Appleby with unflawed respect. 'Eight thousand quid for "Autumn Woods", and you talk about peanuts?'

'It was called that?'

'"Autumn Woods" – and signed "Jos. Reynolds", bottom right.' Unexpectedly, Mr Meatyard roared with laughter. 'I don't deny, mark you, that eight thousand quid hurt a little. And that being had for a sucker hurt a good deal more. But you're not going to leave this house believing that I don't see the joke. Would you say, now, that we might have a drink on it?'

Appleby, although not very anxious for another drink before dinner, would have been churlish to decline this proposal. Mr Meatyard rose and toddled – physically, he had a slight resemblance to Mr Hildebert Braunkopf – to what appeared to be an impeccable piece of eighteenth-century cabinet work in the Chinese taste. He pushed something – perhaps the head or tail of a curly golden dragon – and an impressive array of bottles and glasses was instantly revealed, bathed in a tasteful pinkish light. Appleby almost expected his host to roar with laughter again, since this contraption appeared so clearly to date from the pre-aesthetic period of the Meatyard life-style. Mr Meatyard, however, merely poured gin and vermouth with an anxious and precise attention to the proportions in which his guest signified that his pleasure lay.

'"Minor victim",' Mr Meatyard said, returning to his chair. 'Could we get that clear?'

'The set-up that took you in, Mr Meatyard, involved a certain outlay, as you can see. What might be called research, to begin with, in order to find a gull.'

'A what, Sir John?'

'A gull – old-fashioned word for a dupe. Then there was the studio, or supposed studio, and the stuff exhibited in it. There was the getting in and out of it in a way that would leave the fewest possible traces if you cut up really rough, and the police pitched in their resources in a big way. All that would take time, wouldn't you agree? And time is money.'

'That's a true word.' Mr Meatyard had nodded appreciatively. 'Many's the time I tell it to my younger men. "Lads," I say, "time's brass". You have something there, Sir John.'

'So a mere £8,000 gross was not all that large a figure. Or not for the class of criminal we're dealing with. I don't want to sound disparaging, Mr Meatyard. But in the series of frauds I'm investigating, yours must be regarded as comparatively small beer.'

'Is that so?' Not unnaturally, there was some indignation distinguishable in Mr Meatyard's tone. 'Not really rating, perhaps, for the top-level attention of you folks?'

'Come, sir – you can't quite say that. Not after saying yourself that you'd parted with no more than a few five-pound notes. But there's something I must make clear. I'm not inquiring into this matter in any official way. My days as a policeman are behind me.'

'Do you mean that somebody has hired you as a private detective?'

'I'm afraid it hasn't occurred to anybody to do that.'

'Then you're acting out of pure curiosity?' A slight impatience had come into Mr Meatyard's voice. 'Of course, it's a great pleasure to meet you, Sir John. But, all the same –'

'I'd rather call it a sporting interest. A match at long odds, you might say.'

'Well, of course, that's another matter.' Mr Meatyard spoke with revived interest. 'I'm always ready for a bit of sport. Or a bit of a flutter, as you might say. Martha and I usually look in on the tables when we go to the Riviera. And why not? A little of it never did any harm to those that can afford it. Are you saying that those crooks might be uncommonly hard to catch?'

'Just that. I have a line on several of their jobs – but they stretch over quite a term of years, and fresh clues will be difficult to find. But something might be done, it seems to me, if we put our heads together. A man of your well-known abilities, Mr Meatyard, would be a formidable opponent.'

'But we'd need Martha too.' Mr Meatyard had spoken suddenly and incisively. 'And here she is.'

Chapter Nine

Sir John Appleby was presented to Mrs Meatyard in form, and the lady provided by her husband with a rum and blackcurrant. She was a comfortable woman, whom one would not have supposed given to the ready expression of emotion. Nevertheless her expression kindled promisingly – Appleby thought – as soon as the purpose of his visit was made clear to her.

'I never did want the thing dropped,' she said, 'but Albert is always too considerate. He couldn't bear the thought of our friends poking Charlie at me. I don't deny but what they would have. You know what friends are.'

'At both of us,' Mr Meatyard said. 'But I tell Martha it was business instinct, Sir John – and it's business instinct that has made me what I am. Very bad for business indeed, is being laughed at. I've seen it time and again.'

'But Albert shouldn't have concealed that he lost all that money. Has he shown you "Autumn Woods"?'

'Not yet.'

'Albert, and not me, will have to do the showing of it to you. We keep it in the chauffeur's lavatory at the back of the house. I had it valued, Sir John, just to make quite sure. It was before Albert and I had taken our fancy to pictures, and of course we were that ignorant you wouldn't believe.'

'Your first response to "Autumn Woods", Mrs Meatyard, was one of admiration and pleasure?'

'I dare say I thought it very pretty.' Mrs Meatyard glanced at Appleby with faint amusement, and it was clear that she was far from being a stupid woman. 'But when we found out about 1792 –'

'1792?'

'About Sir Joshua having died then. It's been a joke between

Albert and me ever since. "1792", we say to each other. Well, when we knew just how badly we'd been cheated, I had a dealer to come and look at the thing. He said nothing. Very much the gentleman, he was, and so the situation embarrassed him. Then, point blank, I asked him what he'd give me for "Autumn Woods", frame and all. At that he caught my eye, you might say, and that seemed to cheer him up.'

'Martha has a way with people,' Mr Meatyard said. 'She learned to get along with the highest in the land a tidy time before I did.'

'"Fifteen shillings, Mrs Meatyard," he said to me. So I gave him a stiff tot of Albert's best whisky, and we had a good laugh together. Not that it was all that of a joke, if you ask me – seven thousand nine hundred and ninety-nine pounds five shillings wasn't. Of course, to this day Albert makes light of it. "Plenty more where *that* came from," he says. Not that Albert doesn't know the value of money, Sir John. He was a fine up-standing lad, as you can guess. But I made sure his head was screwed on the right way before I married him.'

'It was very prudent of you.' The Meatyards were north-country folk, and Appleby was coming to feel much at home with them. 'You'd still like to see the thief – for he was a thief, and nothing else – be caught up with and meet his deserts?'

'Maybe, Sir John – although I think I'd hardly call myself a vindictive woman. Mostly, it's just that I'd like the thing explained to me – made a bit of sense of. I don't like unsolved mysteries.'

'No more do I.' Appleby, like the gentleman who had come to value 'Autumn Woods', found Mrs Meatyard cheering him up. 'But just where do you think the chief mystery in the thing lies?'

'In all that about Sir Joshua.' Mrs Meatyard's reply was convinced and immediate. 'It was no joke, as I've said. A plan to go after £8,000 isn't a joke. But the part about Sir Joshua was. You see what I mean?'

'I think I do.' Appleby looked seriously at this admirable woman. 'But will you explain?'

'It's something I can hear, Sir John. On an inner ear, as you might say. And I can see it, too. In one of those clubs in Pall

Mall. Two or three idle upper-class men – the kind Albert and I meet at the banquets of the livery companies – with half a skinful of liquor in them. And one of them says to the others: "I'll wager you I can find a well-heeled character in the City of London so damned ignorant that he can be persuaded to have his wife's portrait painted by Sir Joshua Reynolds". And another of them says: "Done! But deuced hard times, old boy. Shall we make it a dozen of Moët et Chandon '59" Sir John, can *you* hear that?'

'Yes, Mrs Meatyard, I can.'

'Martha,' Mr Meatyard said, 'has uncommon power of mind. If she'd gone into cost accountancy, there would have been no stopping her.'

'But it doesn't seem to connect up with the £8,000.' Mrs Meatyard, with a certain air of homely connoisseurship, took a sip at her rum and blackcurrant. 'You see what I mean? Going after £8,000 is sensible enough, whether criminally or otherwise. But relying on Albert and Martha Meatyard's not knowing that Sir Joshua Reynolds is dead belongs to what you might call a world of pure fun. Why shouldn't they have said Kokoschka or Coldstream or Sutherland? Supposing they put through the whole fraud quick enough, there would have been far less risk in that. So we have a hard-bottomed fraud –'

'Martha,' Mr Meatyard said, 'never minces her words.'

'We have a hard-bottomed fraud and a typical old-fashioned gentlemanly practical joke queerly mixed up. It annoys me, Sir John. I'd gladly find another £8,000 myself just for the explanation of it.' Mrs Meatyard checked herself. For the first time, she seemed momentarily confused. 'I always say things wrong,' she said. 'But Albert has taught me my way around. You won't think, Sir John, that I'm offering *you* a cheque.'

'I've already assured your husband that I haven't turned private detective.' Appleby found himself taking yet further satisfaction in the Meatyards. 'But, Mrs Meatyard, what about that dozen of Moët et Chandon? I get it if I clear up this affair, and you get it if I don't?'

'Not that at all. We'll simply have one of those large bottles – a magnum, isn't it called? – between us if you succeed. But only, of course, if Lady Appleby sometimes comes to town.'

'Nous,' Mr Meatyard said happily. 'What the classical Greeks and Romans called nous. Martha has it.'

'But there is one idea that has occurred to me,' Mrs Meatyard went on. 'There's no great harm in a joke. So until the moment that what you're up to can be proved *not* a joke, there's not all that trouble coming to you if you're found out. It's not criminal to shake hands with Albert and call yourself Sir Joshua Reynolds. It's not even criminal to lead Albert round a lot of worthless pictures and assure him they're masterpieces. So you've done nothing criminal until the very last phase of your plot.'

'Collecting,' Mr Meatyard said, '£8,000 for "Autumn Woods", signed "Jos. Reynolds", bottom right.'

'There's a great deal in what you say.' Appleby looked thoughtfully at Mrs Meatyard. A woman with so sound a head was likely to have an accurate memory as well. 'But about one thing I'm not very clear. Precisely how did the whole thing begin? Wasn't there something about an advertisement?'

'It began with that, all right. "Eminent portrait painter accepts commissions under conditions of confidence".' Mrs Meatyard finished her rum and blackcurrant. 'We didn't realize that it sounded a bit off. In such a high class of newspaper too, it was.'

'It has rather a curious ring. You or your husband just happened to notice it?'

'No, it wasn't like that. And there, Sir John, is the one point at which I criticize Albert. He was at the golf club, and it seems they got talking about having their wives painted. Boasting about it, I shouldn't be surprised. And somebody thrust this advert under Albert's nose. Only he couldn't afterwards at all remember who.'

'That's certainly a very great pity indeed.' Appleby found himself regarding Mr Meatyard with sober reproach. 'You're *sure* it was like that? You didn't simply decide not to be able to remember – because you didn't want the joke going the rounds at the club?'

'Honest to God, Sir John.' Mr Meatyard had actually blushed. 'We'd all had a couple, if the truth be told.'

'Albert is very temperate,' Mrs Meatyard said. 'Very temperate indeed. But you know what gentlemen are after golf. He brought the advert home with him, and we answered it that evening.'

'And then?'

'Well, this young man called, explaining he was acting as an agent. Very well spoken, he was.'

'Could you say just *how* well spoken?'

'It struck me he was a cut above what you might call that kind of errand. And trying to hide the fact.'

'I see. As it happens, that interests me quite a lot. It chimes with a rather similar occasion I've been hearing about. And he explained this business of confidential commissions?'

'Yes, he did. And it seemed to turn out quite respectable and above board.' Mrs Meatyard considered. 'Or *almost* above board.'

'You had come to think there might be something disreputable about it?'

'I had,' Mr Meatyard said. 'It wasn't what would occur to a woman with a refined mind like Martha. But I thought this fellow might paint a man's fancy girls – see?' For a moment Mr Meatyard was unashamedly vulgar. 'And in the altogether, perhaps – or something even rather less nice than that.'

'No doubt it was a reasonable supposition.' Appleby thought fleetingly of Nanna and Pippa. 'But this apprehension proved unfounded?'

'It was a straight business matter.' Mr Meatyard had recovered his poise as a pillar of commercial society. 'It seemed that this eminent portrait painter had gone on contract on exclusive terms. Mark you, I found out later – when I took up the whole subject, as I said – that something of the kind might be true enough. Some pretty big names among the painters do just that: undertake to work full-time over a period of years for one dealer only. Well, that was what we were told this chap had done. But he was looking round for an outside job or two on the quiet. And he was willing to offer attractive terms.'

'Of course we pricked up our ears at that,' Mrs Meatyard said. 'After all, brass is brass.'

'Most certainly it is.' Appleby, who had brought up a fair-sized family on a professional income, found no difficulty in agreeing with this. 'But there were other conditions?'

'It would have to be kept quiet about for two or three years. In particular, we mustn't mention the artist's name.'

'Which turned out,' Mr Meatyard said cheerfully, 'to be Sir Joshua Reynolds. "I'm sure you've heard of him," the young man said to us. It must have been his big moment.'

'It must, indeed. He might have found himself being kicked out of your house there and then. But he saw that he'd got away with it, and he advised you to ring up some picture dealer in Bond Street?'

'Yes – a classy place I'd noticed in passing often enough. He told me just what to ask. What might I expect to have to give for a first-class portrait by Reynolds. Just that. And the answer I got didn't half stagger me, I must say. But, of course, there was to be this cut-price element because of its being done on the Q.T. So I agreed to explore the matter further. And this young man and I went off in a taxi together to call on Sir Joshua. Rich – eh, Sir John? Enough to make a man laugh till his sides ache.'

'I admit that it has its funny aspect.' Making this discreet reply, Appleby found himself in fact overtaken by laughter of a quite immoderate sort. And this proved to be infectious. Whether or not the Meatyards had at one time been liable to wake up in the night and blush all over at the thought of their folly, they commanded a wholly agreeable attitude to it now.

'1792', Mrs Meatyard said, recovering.

'1792', Mr Meatyard echoed. 'And when I came home, it was with –' Less controlled than his wife, Mr Meatyard found himself unable to go on.

'It was with "Autumn Woods" under your arm,' Appleby said. 'And signed by Jos. Reynolds, bottom right.'

'And now we come to the *atelier* of the artist.' Mr Meatyard, who had sunk back in his chair after failing to persuade Appleby to another drink, chuckled reminiscently. 'Not what the French call an *atelier libre*, although I've no doubt I expected that. A nude girl holding a tambourine, and long-haired fellows strolling in and out with sketch-books, in what they call a haze of tobacco-smoke.'

'I see that you had already read,' Appleby said, 'about *la vie de Bohême*.'

'*Trilby*, eh?' Mr Meatyard was delighted. 'And the *quartier latin*. Of course, I've run over all that since taking up pictures. But this place was a surprise, I don't mind telling you. In Mayfair, and done up regardless. Mind you, some things were as you would expect. Sir Joshua had uncommonly long hair, and a velvet jacket covered with dabs of paint. Very old-world, he was – very old-world and courteous. But affable as well. And courtesy and affability don't always go together, let me tell *you*.'

'I've often noticed it,' Appleby said. 'But, of course, he'd be affable as well as courteous – wouldn't he? – when he was after £8,000. By the way, how old would you say Sir Joshua was? Another youngish man, like his emissary?'

'Oh, dear me – no.' Mr Meatyard shook his head. 'Silver hair, and had to walk around with the help of a stick. A gold-headed stick, it was. He told me it had been given him by the King of Spain.'

'There isn't a King of Spain.'

'Ah, but long ago. When he was young, and his talent was first being noticed. He was called to Madrid to paint the Infanta. I remember wondering if the Infanta was a hospital or a cathedral.' Mr Meatyard chuckled luxuriously. 'Well, I've seen what's to be seen in the Prado and the Escorial since then. Sir Joshua – the real Sir Joshua – is small beer, Sir John, when you get to know Velazquez. I recommend Velazquez to you.'

'I must certainly get to know him, some time.' Appleby produced this with proper gravity. 'And then Sir Joshua showed you round his studio?'

'Yes – and there were stacks of paintings. Not in frames, you know, but scattered around against the walls. Portraits, mostly. He told me that what he really liked doing was landscapes, particularly wooded ones. But he hadn't much time to follow his private inclination, so he supposed the landscapes would have a certain scarcity value one day. He hunted around to show me one or two – and, sure enough, there didn't seem many of them. Autumn was what he really liked, he said. And a little after that – quite by chance, you might say, his hand fell on "Autumn Woods" I've never been one to be afraid of speaking up, Sir John. So I asked him for his figure, and offered him cash down. He acted like a perfect gentleman of the older sort – the sort, I've always noticed, who make no bones about money. "Eight thousand," he said – just like that. So it was a deal. And when I'd fixed up about Martha's sittings, I walked out the owner of "Autumn Woods".'

'You must look at it before you go.' Mrs Meatyard made this reiterated suggestion an occasion for standing up; she was competently resolved, Appleby supposed, that her husband's dinner-hour should not be interfered with even by the most eminent of retired policemen. 'But, first, there's one question I'd like to ask you, Sir John. Just how have you come to interest yourself in our experience?'

'It was brought to my notice at the time it happened, Mrs Meatyard, although it wasn't my business actually to carry out an investigation. And now – as I have explained to your husband – it turns out to be only one in a series of frauds connected with works of art of one sort or another.'

'And to be quite small beer among them.' Mr Meatyard interjected this with morose satisfaction. 'Sir John tells me I've been a minor victim. Which suggests there have been some super-Charlies, if you ask me.'

'I see.' Mrs Meatyard's intelligent gaze was directed for a moment very thoughtfully upon Appleby. 'When £8,000 is a minor matter, it must be really large-scale crime that is in question?'

'Bigger rackets go on, Mrs Meatyard. Still, "large-scale crime" is fair enough.'

'I suppose you are accustomed to such things, Sir John, and able to take them lightly. Can they be taken *too* lightly? Not that Albert and I haven't been at fault ourselves, perhaps, in rather making a joke of it all. And we've only been able to do that because – as there's no denying – Albert is a wealthy man now. In a way, of course, it *was* a joke. We've talked about that already. Were any of the other frauds like that, Sir John?'

'Yes. Or at least it is safe to say that there is an element of the freakish in all of them.'

'They were thought of by what must be called a freakish mind?'

'Decidedly.'

'And about a freakish mind there is always something unpredictable?'

'Essentially so, I suppose.' Appleby was beginning to find something vaguely disturbing in this inquisition.

'So far, I take it, nobody can honestly be said to have suffered through these frauds? *Really* suffered, I mean?'

'Well, no. Nobody has been put in any danger of missing his next day's dinner, Mrs Meatyard.'

'Which is why we talk about bets, and champagne, and a sporting interest. The whole thing is simply an amusing puzzle, Sir John, which you have taken it into your head you are going to work out?'

'I don't think I am able to quarrel with that analysis.'

'Martha,' Mr Meatyard said, 'has a very analytical mind. I've been at her to sit on a board or two often enough. But she believes that a woman's sphere is the home.'

'But suppose this joker's jokes caught up with him,' Mrs Meatyard said. 'What would happen then?'

'It's a question,' Mr Meatyard said. 'It's a real question. He's been playing for high stakes – hasn't he? – if £8,000 is peanuts to him. He might turn nasty, if you ask me. Have you considered that, Sir John?'

'I don't believe I have.' Appleby found himself uncertain whether to be amused or impressed. 'But it's a possibility I'll bear in mind from now on. And now, I must really take my leave. But not before seeing "Autumn Woods". And I'd like, of course, to see your Cézanne and your Gainsboroughs as well.'

Part Two

Three Visits

Chapter Ten

Sir Thomas Carrington, of Monks Amble in the County of Northamptonshire, Bart., was by temperament something of a recluse. Moreover the disposition had been growing on him with the years. He had lately abandoned hunting, for example, as an impossibly gregarious pursuit, requiring a quite literal rubbing shoulders with a rabble of upstart townees. It was true that the M.F.H. was his brother-in-law, and because of this he was constrained to permit the meet's being held once or twice in the season before the windows of Monks Amble itself. But he always caused the shutters to be closed for the occasion, and by leaving ostentatiously bare the flag-pole on the west turret of his residence he intimated, at least to the adequately well-informed, that there was no possibility of his being found at home. He had turned shooting into a solitary occupation – much to the indignation of sundry neighbours who in former times had been welcome to turn up with a gun. Even so, Sir Thomas distinctly preferred fishing, since it called only for imitation flies and not for real dogs. It was indeed averred by the devout of the parish (Monks Amble with Toddle Canonicorum) that this reclusive squire was most exact in his weekly attendance at divine service. But as the Carrington family pew stood ten feet high, and was entered through a door giving directly upon Monks Amble park, this appeared a claim impossible of substantiation. There were even ribald and disaffected persons who declared it to be a myth unscrupulously fabricated for the edification of the village.

So much Bobby Appleby had gathered from his father on the occasion of being given his present odd commission. And it really *was* rather odd. He had gone home for the week-end with some notion of running his father over to Keynes Court – and had promptly been handed this minor reconnaissance all on his own. Sir Thomas Carrington was the man who – quite some time ago – might or might not have been defrauded of a genuine Stubbs. Bobby was to beard Sir Thomas and learn all about it.

Bobby's views on a career were as yet of a somewhat negative order. He was quite clear that he did not propose to become a policeman. Unlike the Church or the Army or the Law (he obscurely felt), it was not a thing that ought to run in families. One Appleby at the top of that tree was enough; he himself was going to find another one. Perhaps not a tree at all. Just a shrub. For the fact that one wasn't at all thick – was quite a long way from that, it seemed – didn't at all guarantee that one was going to shoot up in the world But at least he wasn't taking what might be called a vocational test now. It must simply be that his father had thought it would amuse him.

He stopped his car, and surveyed the countryside, map in hand. The church on the horizon was Aldwinkle All Saints, and the poet Dryden had been born in its rectory. Dryden's grandfather had been a baronet, and his next-door neighbour in the baronetcy had no doubt been a Carrington. Perhaps Sir Thomas could be chatted up with a little literary stuff of that kind. But it didn't seem likely. The fine arts might be more promising. But then Sir Thomas was probably a bit touchy on that ground, on account of having lost his Stubbs. Shooting would probably be better. Or Bobby could even try Dryden, and then nip on to shooting if Dryden proved no go. There was a natural transition, come to think of it. One of Dryden's successors as poet laureate had been a harmless country gentleman called Thomas Pye. Pye had written a poem called *The Progress of Refinement,* but hadn't made an awful lot of the theme. So he had fallen back on more native interests. His second poem had been called just *Shooting* – which had been splendidly simple, if nothing else. Perhaps Sir Thomas Carrington would relish a little talk about Pye ... Bobby frowned gloomily. If that was the sort of notion Oxford put into his head, then Oxford was doing little more than make him addle-pated. Nobody would suffer a total stranger to walk in on him and start an instructive harangue on the English poets laureate. There was nothing for it, Bobby saw, but to drive up to Monks Amble and trust to the spur of the moment. And there the house was: an uncompromisingly square Georgian box in the middle-distance. It seemed very much exposed to the elements. It would have been less intimidating, somehow, if decently screened by a few plantations. Bobby shoved into gear, and drove on.

There was a drive, with elaborate wrought-iron gates and a lodge. The gates were locked, but the lodge appeared to be inhabited. Bobby rather supposed that, in this situation, one simply sat back and sounded one's horn. Or was that wrong? Did one get out of one's car, knock at a door, and make affable noises to anybody who chose to appear? Bobby didn't know. They didn't run to anything of the sort at Dream, and although Bobby had a reasonable acquaintance among dwellers in country houses they none of them had any notion of living behind locked gates. Being, however, a resourceful youth, he presently hit on a plan for avoiding plain solecism, either way. He got out of his car and found a door. It proved to have a bell, and on this he contrived to ring a moderate but not ineffectively diffident peal. The door opened almost at once, and an old woman peered out at him.

'I'm terribly sorry,' Bobby said engagingly, 'but I seem to have lost my way. Can you by any chance tell me how to get to Monks Amble – Sir Thomas Carrington's house?'

'You have got. It's here.'

'I say, what luck!' Bobby registered gratified astonishment. 'Would you mind opening the gates?'

'Be you the lad that's to clean out cesspool?'

'I'm afraid I'm not.' Bobby was rather gratified, if anything, at having this lowly status suggested for him, since he shared with a whole generation of privileged English youth a vague aspiration after classlessness.

'Then you mun go away again. It's only the lad for the cesspool that's to be let in.'

'But I want to call on Sir Thomas.'

'Then you mun keep on wanting. Sir Thomas don't want to see 'ee.'

'But that's absurd! Surely, my dear lady' – Bobby found that he had almost said 'my good woman', but his principles had prevailed in time – 'you can't *know* that Sir Thomas doesn't want to see me? You know nothing about me.'

'No more do Sir Thomas, like enough. Not that it would

help if he did.' The old woman began to close the door, as if the business that had called her to it had been satisfactorily concluded. Bobby felt that some emergency procedure was called for, and he had an idea that ruthless prevarication was probably the right thing in an efficient detective.

'As it happens,' he said shamelessly, 'I am a relation of Sir Thomas's. You've probably heard him speak of me – his nephew, Robert.' Bobby felt that this would sound more convincing with a little superadded detail. 'Back from Canada,' he said, 'on a short and unexpected visit.'

'A relation?' The old woman opened the door a little wider, but this didn't prove to be for the purpose of any warmer welcome. 'So much the worse. Sir Thomas, he don't receive the county. And Sir Thomas, he don't receive the local gentry either. But when it comes to relations, be they his own or be they her late ladyship's, Sir Thomas, he gets out his gun.' The door shut with a bang in Bobby's startled face. Then, unexpectedly, it momentarily opened again. 'Except,' the old woman said, 'that sometimes he do prefer a dog-whip.'

This time, the door closed for good.

So Bobby Appleby climbed back into his car. He wondered darkly how much his father had gathered about the domestic life of Sir Thomas Carrington, and whether he had himself been sent on this mission as a species of poor family joke. But he certainly wasn't going to go home now, leaving Sir Thomas uninterviewed – not even if the alternative meant risking atrocious assault. Bobby had never been peppered with pellets, and a dog-whip was not among the fairly numerous instruments with which he had been corrected at one or another school. He could only live and learn.

He might, of course, simply climb over a wall or fence, or push through a hedge. But he was going to drive up to Monks Amble in proper style if he could. Probably there would be less imposing entrances, designed for one or another sort of rural traffic with the great house, which nobody bothered to lock. Behind the mansion, indeed, and at no more than a modest remove from it, was a small huddle of buildings which might be a home farm. He consulted his map again. It said, sure enough,

Monks Amble Manor Farm. Bobby started the engine and skirted the small park. Within a couple of minutes he was among stables. And from these there was no difficulty in driving round to the front of the house.

It occurred to him to hope that the old woman in the lodge wasn't equipped with a telephone; that she hadn't, repenting her uncivil behaviour, rung up Sir Thomas to say how reluctantly she had turned away a wandering nephew from Canada. But that was absurd, and so had the whole notion of false pretences been. He would simply have a go under his own colours. The house, now that he was close up to it, seemed rather reassuring; it had a respectable and well-cared for look that didn't suggest habitation by a ferocious eccentric. Only the scene did a little lack animation. Bobby would have liked to see a housemaid circumspectly gossiping with a gardener's boy through an open window, or even just a couple of contented spaniels lazing by the front door. But nothing of the sort was visible. He got out of his car and rang a bell. It was answered by a manservant who didn't look too promising. He might have been younger brother, indeed, to the old woman in the lodge.

'Good morning,' Bobby said. 'Is Sir Thomas –'

'Not at home.'

There is always a daunting absoluteness about these conventional words. Very little can be achieved in face of them. One can leave a visiting-card (supposing one to have so archaic an object about one's person). One can claim the right to sit down in a man's hall and scribble him a note. One can't – or not on any purely social assumption – say firmly, 'I'll wait'. Bobby felt at an impasse. Unlike the old woman, Sir Thomas's butler was too well-trained positively to close the door before the caller had turned away. On the other hand, he appeared to acknowledge no obligation to further utterance. Bobby felt that a decisive move on his own part was required, even if it meant breaking his recent resolution to avoid prevarication.

'But I've come about the cesspool,' Bobby said.

'Then get into it.'

'But I have to see Sir Thomas first.' Bobby, although inwardly aghast at having plunged into this further piece of nonsense, spoke confidently. 'I have to take his instructions, you see, before preparing an estimate.' He looked past the butler and into the recesses of a large and murky hall as he thus piled fib on fib. For a moment he thought he glimpsed a moving figure – and even what might have been a human face behind an enormous moustache. Then he heard a noise. It was a very familiar noise indeed. He made it himself whenever he slipped a couple of cartridges into the old 12-bore he had inherited from an uncle. In his present circumstances, he didn't like the sound at all. He would willingly have swopped it even for a sinister preliminary crack of a whip. Still, he wasn't going to be intimidated. 'So will you please,' he said, 'tell your master I am here?'

The butler had been disconcerted – which was something. But at this his eyes narrowed suspiciously. Perhaps, Bobby thought, 'your master' had been a false note. It was probably not a locution employed by persons in the cesspool business. And it was this point that the butler now took up. He comprehended Bobby's clothes and his hair-cut, his complexion and his finger-nails, in a single professional and sombrely sceptical glance.

'You don't look like a young man who has come about the drains,' the butler said. 'You look more like a college lad, if you ask me.'

'But I *am* a college lad. I mean, I've *been* a college lad. An honours degree in sanitation is essential for the cesspool business now. I got mine at Oxford. Please take Sir Thomas my name. It's Appleby.'

At this, rather surprisingly, Sir Thomas Carrington's butler took half a step into the open air. This appeared to be for the purpose of scrutinizing Bobby in a better light.

'You wait here.' Something had emerged, Bobby felt, to shake the butler into this wholly irregular formula – one permissible at the portals only of altogether humbler domiciles. Bobby, left standing on the doorstep, did his best to use his ears. It might be vital to manage a timely skip behind one of the bleak Doric pillars which flanked Sir Thomas's front door. But neither shotgun nor dog-whip gave any further indication of its existence. Instead, a muttered colloquy made itself heard. Bobby fancied he distinguished – very perplexingly – the word 'Twickenham'. Even more strangely, the same voice said something about 'injury time', and the butler distinctly enunciated the phrase, 'far out on the twenty-five'. And then the butler was back again. He was carrying what was instantly identifiable as a not very recent copy of the *Illustrated London News*. He halted in the doorway; he looked at this organ of the press; he looked at Bobby. 'It would be Mr *Robert* Appleby?' he asked.

'That's right. My father –' Bobby broke off. His mind (although lately coming to be reported upon so agreeably by his tutors) was susceptible to moments of confusion. This was one of them. That his name was known at Monks Amble could only be the consequence, he supposed, of some further deplorable family joke.

'It's him, all right!' The butler – most confoundingly – had turned and pitched this information, with every appearance of excitement, into the recesses of the hall. 'You come in,' he said, turning back to Bobby. 'And I 'ope you'll permit me to shake you by the 'and.'

That Sir Thomas's butler should be so emotionally disturbed as to have lost command of his aspirates struck Bobby as something portentous in itself. But he had no leisure to reflect on it, since he now found himself in the presence of Sir Thomas. The squire of Monks Amble did have an enormous moustache. But if this was alarming, his posture was reassuring. He was in the act of replacing a shot gun in a rack on the wall. Having accomplished this, he turned round, snatched the *Illustrated London News* from his henchman, gave it a brief confirmatory glance, and advanced upon Bobby with the largest cordiality.

'Absolutely delighted,' Sir Thomas Carrington said. 'Deuced good of you to call. Compare notes, eh? Changed times, of course. Plenty to talk about. Take off your coat. Billington – brandy and cigars.'

Billington vanished. Bobby's wits were still not working quite properly.

'It's awfully kind of you, sir,' he said. 'Decent of you to see me, I mean. I don't think you've actually met my father. He's Sir John Appleby.'

'Never heard of him. Plain K., eh? Not in the baronetage. Don't know him from Adam, I'm afraid. But come into my den, my dear boy. I've one or two things that ought to interest you.'

Bobby found himself led into a small apartment of informal character. It appeared to have been excavated beneath rather an imposing staircase. And its most prominent feature revealed the truth at once. Perched alone on a peg above the chimney-piece was a faded blue velvet cap with a silver tassel. The walls, too, told their story. They were hung with group photographs of innumerable Rugger Fifteens of the past. It was a reasonable conjecture that Sir Thomas Carrington figured in several of them.

'A capital game,' Sir Thomas was saying. 'Billington and I don't go out much, you know. Haven't actually been to Twickenham these half dozen years, I'd say. But, of course, we have it on the box.' Sir Thomas gestured towards a television set in a corner of the room. 'And we don't forget that drop goal of yours, Appleby. We often talk about it. Magnificent effort. In the last thirty seconds, eh? And from pretty well on the touch-line, and back on the twenty-five. Saved the match. I can tell you something rather similar about the game in twenty-seven. But my own Varsity Match was back in twenty-two. Tell you about it after lunch.'

'I'll be awfully interested to hear about it,' Bobby said mendaciously. It had always seemed to him that all Rugger toughs in photographs were virtually indistinguishable one from another, and he didn't see how he himself could conceivably be an exception. Yet Billington had recognized him from a mere memory of just such a photograph in an illustrated paper. Billington as a butler to an obscure country gentleman had quite missed his vocation. He ought to be holding down a key job at Scotland Yard.

'And about Cuppers in twenty-one,' Sir Thomas continued happily. 'I can tell you a lot about that. Though I say it myself, the House fielded a damned good side. A difficult thing to do, with the college cluttered up with all those useless wet-bobs from Eton.'

'I suppose it must have been.' Bobby, although the simplicity of his own earlier college years had inured him to conversation on athletic topics, found himself failing to relish the prospect of sustained tête-à-tête with Sir Thomas. Nor could he at all see how he was going to work round to the pilfered painting. It would be easier if George Stubbs had painted Rugger matches, like Mr Lawrence Toynbee. Unfortunately in Stubbs's time Rugby football hadn't been invented, and football of any sort was thought of as a particularly reprehensible form of plebeian brawling. Bobby had a dim notion that Stubbs had once or twice delineated a cricket match. But there was no sign that Sir Thomas Carrington – or Billington, for that matter – took the slightest interest in cricket.

'I want to talk to you seriously about the handling of the scrum.' Sir Thomas said this as, without consultation, he poured out two alarming measures of brandy. 'Mind you, I don't deny that the science of the game has progressed in a good many ways since my time. But we did know how to wheel. You don't see a modern scrum wheeling the way we did. Cigar? Come to think of it, a pipe's better for the wind.'

'I think I'll just smoke my pipe a little later,' Bobby said modestly. Not to seem disdainful of Sir Thomas's hospitality, he took a sip of the brandy. The result was unexpected and extremely curious. So minute an ingestion of alcohol couldn't conceivably have had any real effect. Yet its mere sting on his palate seemed to snap open a shutter in his mind. 'I'm tremendously interested,' he said, 'in what you say about the scrum. You see, I've sometimes thought about what a scrum-half should know. It's a matter of mechanics, in a way. I mean, there you have eight chaps, all locked together with their shoulders down, and with ever so complex a play of forces going on.'

'Perfectly true.' Sir Thomas nodded sagely – an old Blue listening to a young one.

'A scrum-half is even an artist in his way. Like Michelangelo, or somebody like that. Watching all those muscles at work, and calculating just what effect they're going to produce. So he ought really to have studied anatomy. Of course, some have. Have you noticed, sir, that a good many of the greatest scrum-halves of modern times have been medical students?'

'I don't know that I have.' Sir Thomas was extremely impressed. 'I must have Billington look it up. Most interesting. Anatomy – upon my soul!'

'Take the horse. Everybody studies the anatomy of the horse.'

'Perfectly true, Appleby. We had lectures on it at my private school. Invaluable thing. Remember it all very well. Much better than their Latin and so forth.'

'It's been so for a long time. For two hundred years, I suppose, every gentleman's library has included Stubbs's book.'

'What's that? Stubbs, did you say?' There was a promising alertness in Sir Thomas's voice.

'Of course, he became a painter mainly. But he published his *Anatomy of the Horse* in 1766.' Bobby paused impressively, justly conscious of having done his home-work. 'A most exhaustive study of equine structure. And the basis, really, of a lot of his artistic work. So it seems to me that if scrum-halves –' Bobby managed to pause invitingly – and to his joy Sir Thomas uttered.

'Quite right,' he said. 'Got the book myself – goes without saying. But – do you know? – I could tell you a devilish odd thing about Stubbs.'

'I'd be most awfully interested to hear it.'

But, at this moment, the door of Sir Thomas's den opened, to reveal Billington in a formal posture.

'Luncheon is served,' Billington said.

Chapter Eleven

The interruption might well have been fatal. For one thing, Bobby felt he ought to make noises deprecating the notion of his staying to lunch at all. For another – and when this had been briskly brushed aside – it became evident that Billington was to remain in attendance throughout the meal. It seemed possible that this might exercise an inhibiting effect on the flow of his employer's reminiscences. But nothing of the sort occurred. For Billington was very much a confidential retainer. As well as rivalling Sir Thomas as a connoisseur of Rugby football, it soon appeared that he was something of an oracle on Carrington family history as well.

'Fact is that I possessed a Stubbs,' Sir Thomas said. 'Ought to possess it still. But there was this damned joke. That right, Billington?'

'Well, Sir Thomas, we can't be all that clear. About the picture ever having been genuine for a start, that is. We have to recall your late mother's temperament, in a manner of speaking. And very rum it was, sir, to speak with all respect.'

'Perfectly true.' Sir Thomas paused to consume several spoonfuls of soup – a feat which the character of his moustache rendered one of considerable virtuosity. 'My mother had a very good seat, mark you, and could take her fences with the best of them. But she was certainly rum. Billington – that's a very good word for her. Rum.'

'Thank you, Sir Thomas.'

'Finished in Paris, you know, Appleby. Regular thing. None of those damned Swiss places in her time. But she broke out. With the drawing-master, it seems. And the interest never left her. Always dabbling with her paint-box. Jokes, too. Painted something deuced indecent once – a couple of heathen goddesses quite starkers – and passed it off as by some desperate old Italian.'

'But nudes,' Bobby said, 'aren't really indecent, are they?'

'My dear boy, they are when cooked up by a Victorian baronet's lady. That right, Billington?'

'Undoubtedly, Sir Thomas.'

'So in the end I couldn't be quite certain about this Stubbs. It was my mother who came on it, you see, poking around in the stables.'

'The stables?'

'Right place for a painting of two uncommonly fine Arabs, I'd say. Take the kitchen at Christ Church. Had a splendid painting of a butcher's shop in my day, by some top-ranking painter of the Resurgence.'

'The Renaissance,' Bobby said automatically – for he had lately been tending to pick up some of his tutor's habits.

'That's right. And an inspiration to the college chef, if you ask me. Not there now, I'm told. Shoved into some picture-gallery. Billington, what was I talking about?'

'The unfortunate matter of the George Stubbs, Sir Thomas.'

'So I was. Perhaps we ought to get back to Rugger. Interest you a good deal more – eh, Appleby?'

'I'd like to hear about the end of Stubbs first, sir.'

'Not much to tell. We all liked this picture my mother had found – or said she had found.'

'You were doubtful about that at the time?'

'Lord, no. She was an old woman then, and the notion of one of her jokes never entered our heads.'

'Did your mother say it was by Stubbs?'

'I really don't know, my boy. She may have done. Name wouldn't have conveyed much to us, except perhaps as that of the chap who wrote the book.'

'*The Anatomy of the Horse*? Yes, of course. But what happened then?'

'Nothing at all, until my father died – which was years after the death of my mother, and of my poor wife, too, for that matter. My father lived to a tremendous old age. Billington, I'm right there – eh?'

'Certainly, Sir Thomas. The late Sir Thomas was ninety-six at the time of his regretted decease.'

'Billington knows,' Sir Thomas said with approval. 'Well, when my father died, we had to have fellows in to value things. Probate, you know. Damned iniquitious death-duties. One of them was a picture-wallah. Spotted the Stubbs, and congratulated me on it. Seemed surprised I didn't know the thing meant money.'

'I see. So this chap concluded that it *was* a Stubbs, and valued it accordingly?'

'Just that. Mind you, it seemed a snap job. Didn't scratch at the thing, or anything of that kind. Just took a quick look at it and said "Nice little Stubbs".'

'But how did you come to lose it, Sir Thomas?? Did this man you're telling me about have anything more to do with it?'

'Nothing at all. Billington – that correct?'

'Not exactly, Sir Thomas. The gentleman did suggest that he take away the painting and have it cleaned for you.'

'To be sure, so he did. Reasonable thing, I suppose. Splendid brutes: crests thin, fetlock joints large, shoulders lying well on the chest. Show up better if one got off the dirt.'

'But you didn't let him have it?'

'No, I didn't – although I can't remember why. But yes I can. Billington advised against it. That right, Billington?'

'That is correct, Sir Thomas. If the picture was worth a mint of money, then caution was indicated.'

'Just so. Well, the fellow went away. But he must have told his discovery to some of the top people in his own line. And then they played this joke on me. Queer business. None of us has ever got to the bottom of it – not even Billington. Damned embarrassing, just at the time. Rather forgotten the details now. But Billington knows.'

'I am moderately informed, Sir Thomas.' Billington, who had been in the act of replenishing his employer's glass with brandy (which appeared to be drunk as a matter of course throughout this meal), turned impressively towards Bobby. 'We had a communication, sir, from the President of the Royal Academy –'

'Only we hadn't.' Sir Thomas's memory seemed to have cleared. 'Because it wasn't from him at all.'

'I shall come to that, sir.' Billington was reproachful. 'The letter was about a very 'igh-class show to be held at Burlington 'ouse in London.' Billington paused, as if obscurely aware of having mislaid something. 'Very *high*-class indeed,' he said, 'as all such at Burlington *H*ouse are.'

'So I packed the thing up,' Sir Thomas said, 'and sent it off. Not actually to Burlington House, but to some place where the letter said they were collecting everything.'

'I see,' Bobby said.

'So there you are.' Sir Thomas paused. 'And that brings us to the Varsity Match.'

'To the Varsity Match!' Bobby felt dismay. 'But won't you first –'

'The last that Billington and I went up for. And being in town, I thought we'd drop in on these Royal Academy fellows and have a word about the picture. Billington, carry on.'

'Yes, Sir Thomas. A very courteous secretary, there was. More of a gentleman, in a manner of speaking, than a person moving in hartistic circles. 'e said the Stubbs 'ad never been 'eard of.' The excitement of his narrative was gaining on Billington. 'Well, Sir Thomas wasn't pleased, and rightly so. 'e spoke his mind.'

'So I did.' Sir Thomas appeared delighted by this commendation. 'But fellow was very civil, as Billington says. Turned the place upside-down, and there the damned picture was, after all. Had arrived that morning. Eh, Billington?'

'Yes, Sir Thomas – and with a letter purporting to be from yourself, offering your Stubbs for the exhibition in what might be called an unsolicited way. And at that moment, in comes the President himself. Of the Royal Academy, that's to say. Affable as you please, and with an 'andle to his name.'

'Picked up a K., I suppose, for having painted cabinet ministers.' Sir Thomas chuckled indulgently. 'Nice enough chap.'

'Tactful, I thought 'e was. Clearly some misunderstanding, 'e said, but they'd be delighted to 'ang the Stubbs.'

'Did the President call it a Stubbs?' Bobby asked.

'That, now, I wouldn't swear to. But Sir Thomas's picture

106

would be gratefully accepted, and fortunately there was a place for it in the Gents.'

'The Gents?' Bobby, not unnaturally, was surprised.

'There was to be a small overflow in the Gents.' Billington paused, as if vaguely aware of something wrong with this expression. 'It's a place very much frequented during these shows, it seems. On account of art-lovers being mostly elderly.'

'But that was why there was the outrage.' At this point, Sir Thomas appeared to be surprisingly on the spot. 'If it had been in one of the main galleries, you know, this demonstrating scoundrel, who was after Votes for Women –'

'Banning the Bomb,' Billington said.

'Something of that kind. He'd have been nabbed before he slashed the thing. As it was, the whole affair was deuced awkward. For the Stubbs turned out to have been painted on top of something else. It was made to appear that I'd offered this show a damned fake.'

'As was natural and proper,' Billington said, 'Sir Thomas 'e raised 'ell. Scotland Yard, and all that.'

'But then we thought better of it. Billington's idea, really. He saw we were going to appear damned fools. Better to call off the coppers, and let be. Well, that's the story.'

Luncheon with Sir Thomas Carrington had come virtually to its end. Bobby Appleby glanced dubiously at something like two inches of brandy still in the glass before him. He had to keep a clear head to sort all this out. He also had to drive a car. But Billington had turned aside to prepare coffee, and for a moment Sir Thomas was obscurely occupied with his moustache. In the middle of the table was a small bowl of anemones. Bobby deftly tipped his brandy into it, and then raised his glass with great ostentation to his lips. Sir Thomas, glancing up, noted with approval a young man capable of gulping spirits a gill at a time.

'Another drop of brandy?' Sir Thomas said.

'No, thank you very much – but I've enjoyed it enormously.'

'Another stiff tot, dear boy, might go very well with that long chat we're going to have about the scrum.'

'Or Benedictine,' Billington suggested hospitably. 'Or we have a very nice Green Chartreuse.'

'I think I'd rather not.' Bobby spoke quite nervously. It seemed to him that something was happening to the anemones. He could have sworn that they were changing colour and stirring drunkenly. 'It looks – doesn't it? – as if there's no telling whether there was ever a real Stubbs or not.'

'One is aware of alternative hypotheses, sir.' Billington articulated these words with prudent precision. 'Either the late Sir Thomas's lady was having a bit of a joke in the first place, or there was a proper Stubbs and it vanished between this and Burlington' – Billington paused impressively – 'House.'

'That's it,' Sir Thomas said, and his glance wandered across the table. 'Nice flowers these, eh? Striking colours.'

'Lovely,' Bobby said, his nervousness increasing. He realized that, from Sir Thomas Carrington's point of view, the topic of the Stubbs had exhausted itself. And clearly a great deal of talk about Rugger was going to follow. Having been given a very decent lunch in the expectation of this, he couldn't with any honesty now think to cut and run for it. And Rugger, after all, still interested him quite a lot. But it did seem important to make at least one further bid for any remaining facts about the picture business that might be lurking either in Sir Thomas's mind or in Billington's. Bobby tried to think of the sort of questions his father would ask. Perhaps there was some single and vital question that hadn't occurred to him. It would be very annoying to return to Dream and almost immediately have his father saying incredulously, 'You mean to say you didn't ask *that*?' Perhaps he had been rash to feed all that brandy to the anemones. Perhaps one additional swig at it would have produced inspiration. 'About the fellow who came to value your pictures,' he heard himself say. 'He wanted to take away the Stubbs – if it was a Stubbs – and have it cleaned for you. Do you remember anything else about him?'

'Don't want to remember him at all, my dear lad.' Sir Thomas sounded impatient, but checked himself. 'Not that he seemed at all a bad fellow. Gent, and all that. And went up in the world shortly afterwards. That right, Billington?'

'Yes, Sir Thomas. You remarked it in *The Times*. What they call the University News, it was in. And it was Oxford or Cambridge he went to, not one of the modern hestablishments. Very well-spoken, 'e was – very well-spoken and polite. Name of Sans-bury, I remember.' Billington turned to Bobby. 'Ever heard of him, sir? An intellectual, 'e was. Mightn't be your type.'

'I've heard of him my father, as a matter of fact.' Bobby noticed that the anemones, their phase of inebriation over, were now curling up exhausted. Bobby felt rather exhausted too. But he braced himself, and turned to Sir Thomas. 'And now about handling the scrum,' he said.

Chapter Twelve

Judith Appleby had discovered that, in a distant fashion, she was a relation of Lady Canadine. It was something she was frequently able to do – for the simple reason that her family, the Ravens, had through several generations been of a strikingly prolific habit, and had married all over the place. And *Who's Who* had revealed that Lady Canadine (wife of the former owner of an improper garden ornament) had been a Raven. The thing was as simple as that. A remote Raven, but a Raven, all the same.

Unfortunately this tenuous consanguinity didn't look like taking her very far. She couldn't recall ever having met either of the Canadines, so the dim fact would scarcely licence a casual call. Moreover if Bobby was going to face some difficulty in manoeuvring Sir Thomas Carrington into being communicative about an entirely innocent painting by George Stubbs, she wasn't herself likely to find it any easier to broach with an elderly female of conventional mind (as Lady Canadine, she felt, was sure to be) an affair turning upon anything so indelicate as the purloined statue. It was true that Judith herself was by profession a sculptor, and there might be something in that. Could she, for example, simply drive up to Netherway (which was the Canadines' house) and announce that she had heard of the fame of a particularly fine Graeco-Roman work in the possession of the family? She doubted it. Her technical interest in such objects would be best kept in reserve.

And there was another difficulty. The Canadines were the only people who hadn't made at least some degree of public fuss about their loss. Lord Canadine's noble friend, Lord Cockayne; Sir Thomas Carrington, a pillar of the landed gentry; Mr Meatyard, equally a pillar of the higher mercantile class; Mr Hildebert Braunkopf, that bastion of the refined ethical conscience in the picture-trade: all these (before, so to speak, losing their nerve) had ventilated their deprivations to the police. But Canadine appeared to have done no more than mention his embarrassing loss among his private friends. Cockayne had known about it, and it was only through him that the Appleby's had heard of the indecorously animated statue at all. That its owners had elected to be so reticent about its disappearance made any direct inquiry into the affair additionally tricky.

At this point Judith Appleby had abandoned *Who's Who*, and tried *Gardens of England and Wales*. Netherway was celebrated, it seemed, for a large collection of steam engines, very old yew trees, and alpine plants. Alpines, it struck her, were the most likely to be Lady Canadine's concern, so she applied herself to the Alpine Garden Society's *Quarterly Bulletin*. This confirmed her guess. Lady Canadine was an authority on the choicer androsaces and other naturally saxatile plants. Judith was quite good at this sort of language. It was going to be plain sailing, she told herself. And she drove off to Netherway at once.

It was a three-hour drive; if she stopped at a pub for a sandwich, she could make her appearance at a civil hour in the afternoon. And as the little car skimmed over the downs, she could marshall her knowledge of the saxatiles. Did Lady Canadine feel that *Draba mollissima* throve best in tufa holes? She herself had enjoyed modest success in growing *Phyteuma comosum* that way. Her uncle Everard Raven – whom Lady Canadine perhaps remembered – had planted *Chamaecyparis obtusa* nearly seventy years ago, and so dense were these delightful green bun-shaped balls that their spread was no more than twelve or fifteen inches to this day. And how enchantingly slow-growing was the Noah's Ark tree! She had planted one on the birth of each of her children, and the children had always put on five inches to the trees' one. That would be the sort of thing – but produced with a steady deference for Lady Canadine's superior knowledge. For Judith's visit, if it were to be colourable, must be given the character of a pilgrimage.

But although Judith Appleby was interested in gardens she was rather more interested, after all, in sculpture and the history of sculpture. So she found herself beginning to wonder about the piece of garden statuary which Lord Canadine had, it seemed, inherited. She began to wonder about it in the whole context of the series of bizarre frauds and robberies which her husband had described to her. Superficially, it seemed the least odd of these affairs. The simple theft of an object of value was all that was in question – except for the further point that the object had been tastelessly fooled around with by some former owner, and that this had made the publicizing of its loss impolitic. But what *was* odd – and Judith was in no doubt about this – was the existence in anybody's garden, over a long period of time, of an object of high antiquity and great value. According to the account of the matter given to John by Lord Cockayne, the present Lord Canadine had been quite unaware of the statue's value until casually informed of the fact some time after its disappearance. There was nothing impossible about this, but it did seem a little surprising. It might at least be of interest to discover who Canadine's informant had been.

The antiquity of Netherway's yew trees, at least, could not be challenged. They formed gloomy groves in a large park – which was a disposition of things curious in itself. The steam engines (which Judith had vaguely expected to find housed in converted stables, or the like, after the fashion of a private museum) formed rather similar groups and clumps of their own; only as they were freshly painted in the appropriate colours of the railway companies to which, at one time or another in the nineteenth and twentieth centuries, they had severally belonged, the effect they rendered was rather more gay. They might, indeed, have been guests at a garden party; in threes and fours they stood more or less nose to nose, as if exchanging obligatory small-talk with practised ease. Rudyard Kipling, Judith recalled, had been fond of writing fables in which locomotive engines and steamships turned chatty between each other or between their several components. But the effect here was less of that than of *la révolution surréaliste*. A little old-hat, in fact. It was a freakish mind that had perpetrated such a manifestation in an English park.

The Canadines were much less grand than the Cockaynes, and probably a good deal less prosperous as well. The latter fact seemed reflected in the house now coming into view; it was a respectable Queen Anne mansion, but didn't look in the best repair. The grounds, on the other hand, were perfectly tended, and it was already possible to glimpse a formal garden which gave a similar effect.

Judith braked sharply. She had become aware that in front of her was a level-crossing, and that it was closed against her. A little barrier had come down, and a little bell was ringing and a little light was flashing. A moment later, the train appeared. It struck her as belonging to a locomotive world midway between miniature railways and model railways. The elderly man perched on the cab of the engine was quite as big as the engine itself. He was wearing a grey bowler hat. He removed it and bowed gravely to Judith as he went past. The train vanished within one of the clumps of yew trees; the barrier went up; Judith drove on. There could be no doubt that she had been saluted by Lord Canadine.

Lady Canadine was charmed. Or in a dim way she was charmed – for she moved and spoke with a vagueness suggesting that she had in fact withdrawn from a world grown too perplexing long ago, and had left behind only an apparatus of social responses entirely adequate in their way to anything except unexpected exigency. Judith certainly didn't rate as that; Lady Canadine most perfectly comprehended the ramifications of the Ravens, and was charmed to meet a kinswoman – and especially a kinswoman who had heard of her notable success with *Globularia cordifolia* and *Alyssum serpyllifolium*. Lady Canadine had lately been doing a lot with dry walls. But with these the problem, of course, was air pockets. Air pockets harbour slugs.

In discussion of these and similar learned matters, Judith and her involuntary hostess spent an agreeable if slightly trailing hour. Judith ventured to assert the excellence of equal parts of turfy loam, peat, sharp sand and stone chippings. Lady Canadine accepted this, but with the proviso that the sand must come from Bedfordshire. Her husband frequently ordered large quantities of builder's sand – it had something to do with his railway – and thought she ought herself to make do with that. But adequate drainage was almost impossible with builder's sand. Lady Appleby must have discovered that long ago.

Judith murmured diffidently that, on the contrary, this was a most valuable accession to her knowledge of the subject. Inwardly, she reflected that it wasn't, unfortunately, at all the knowledge she had come to collect. She wondered whether she would be asked to stay to tea – and a covert glance at her watch told her she was bound to be. Possibly Lord Canadine himself would be easier to tackle. But Canadine was perhaps the kind of man who didn't turn up at his wife's tea-table; who felt that marital decorum was satisfied by reunion half an hour before dinner. No doubt he had to grease and oil his rolling-stock before tucking it up for the night. And Lady Canadine, correspondingly, would have to make the round of her troughs. Troughs, she had been obliged to confess, were coming to engage more of her regard than even dry walls. There were no air pockets in troughs.

Judith was wondering whether from troughs she could steer the conversation to sarcophagi, and from sarcophagi to sculpture, when Lady Canadine said something which, although not in the least out of the way, alerted her guest instantly.

'I wonder,' Lady Canadine suggested, 'whether you would care to see the water garden?'

'Very much. I am so interested in submerged aquatics. And in marginal aquatics, as well.'

'The formal pond in the sunken garden has very little that is notable at present. But I should like to show you our little series of informal pools in secluded situations. They were designed by my father-in-law many years ago.'

This sounded so promising – at least compared with anything that had been mentioned so far – that Judith found herself quickening her pace. Lady Canadine seemed to find this eagerness commendable, and contrived to move quite briskly herself. When she next spoke, however, it was on a slightly despondent note.

'The margins are so difficult, are they not, with artificial pools? Really attractive aquatics of scrambling habit are not easy to hit upon.'

Judith had hardly had time to agree with this, and to put in a good word for Bog Bean, when the first of what Lady Canadine called the informal pools was before her. It lay at the foot of a steep little gully or ravine which, although unexpected on its particular terrain, seemed itself not to have been artificially constructed. A small stream tumbled down it, and it was by this that the series of pools was fed. This first pool was full of water-lilies of an apple-blossom pink, and Judith duly admired them. But she scarcely heard Lady Canadine remarking instructively that *Marliacea Carnea* has a robust constitution. She had a sudden strong persuasion that – for what the point was worth – she was approaching the modest and retired spot from which Lord Canadine's Graeco-Roman goddess had been ravished away. The second of the pools, certainly, had every title to be called secluded; it was approached by a narrow path which wound upwards between shrubs so unobtrusively that a casual glance might miss it altogether. Here again there was a pause for appropriate remarks. Lady Canadine's impulse of showmanship, however, now showed signs of declining.

'I scarcely think,' she said, 'that you will wish to climb to the third pool. It is really something of a scramble. There was even a time when it was considered quite unsuitable for ladies.'

'How very amusing. But I don't at all feel that I want to decline the challenge. I'm sure the last of these ponds will contain something quite beautiful.'

'It used to be supposed to do so.' Lady Canadine looked almost startled as she said this. She no doubt felt it to have been indiscreet. 'But the path is really *quite* steep. It used to be known as the Gentlemen's Steps.' She paused, but seemed to realize that her newly-discovered relation was not to be deflected. 'I shall lead the way,' she said with resignation.

The difficulty of the Gentlemen's Steps was exaggerated. It could hardly be otherwise in such a situation. And the third pool turned out to be much like those below – except that in the middle of it was an empty stone pedestal, raised some inches above the surface of the water. Judith took one look at it, and felt that the crucial moment had come. It was true that the pool was surrounded by Corkscrew Rush, which it is quite improper not to greet with amused delight. But Judith ignored it. She pointed to the pedestal.

'That must be for a statue or a fountain,' she said firmly. 'What has happened to it?'

There was a moment's silence – for Lady Canadine was simply

looking at her in dumb dismay. Then, from close behind Judith, a man's voice spoke.

'What, indeed?' the voice said. 'I'm afraid we shall never know.'

Chapter Thirteen

When Judith turned round, it was to see a grey bowler hat held courteously in air. The speaker – who must have ascended the Gentlemen's Steps behind them – was Lord Canadine himself. His manner of announcing his presence, although it had been a shade abrupt, failed to disturb his wife's social manner.

'Humphrey, dear,' Lady Canadine said, 'Such a pleasant thing. A visit from a kinswoman of mine, Judith Appleby. I don't think you knew her father. But you must have met her uncle, Everard Raven.'

'Yes, indeed.' Lord Canadine said this with the polite *aplomb* of one who doesn't in the least mean what he says. 'How very nice.' He shook hands briskly, and with a glance that set Judith wondering. Lady Canadine, learned in alpines and aquatics but notably unoppressed by any other intellectual concern, was unlikely to perplex a child. But her husband could not be placed so readily. The proprietor of ever so many superannuated puff-puffs, and of one that actually chugged along a real railway line, ought not to have outlived the innocence of his prep school days. But it was possible that he was eccentric rather than retarded. He might even be a little mad. Perhaps Lady Canadine's air of having closed her account with anything apart from vegetable nature was not unconnected with certain lurking facets of her husband's character. Now he was glancing round the verges of the pool. 'Julia showing you the duckweed, Lady Appleby?' he said with easy jocularity. 'No idea of what that yellow stuff is, I'm afraid.'

'*Jussieua repens.*' Lady Canadine's tone hinted faint reproach. 'So useful because of its creeping habit. And on the other side is False Loosestrife.'

'Doesn't sound as if it should be trusted for a moment. Creeping habit too, I suppose. Like all those confounded trippers. It was they who made away with the statue, you know. Or so I supposed until I was told that it was much more valuable than I'd ever tumbled to. After that, I began to wonder. There's a great deal of professional thieving from places of our sort nowadays, I'm told. A friend of mine lost an elephant that way.'

'How very odd!' It struck Judith that Lord Canadine was at least more entertaining than his wife. 'Do you mean from an estate in Africa?'

'Lord, no. Wiltshire. Old Tommy Cunningham. I expect you know him – Sly Bacon is what we used to call him. He bought this elephant along with a couple of giraffes to give rides to the trippers' kids. Up and down the terrace in front of Waterbath, which is an uncommonly fine Palladian mansion, as I think you'll agree. So it was really a very jolly idea. One likes the picture of it, I must say. But they weren't giraffes, by the way. They were camels. One *can* ride giraffes, but the effect is rather slithery. I'd have liked to think up the elephant and camels myself. But of course I take people for rides on my railway.'

'Did somebody simply lead away the elephant in the night?'

'That was what the police thought at first. They had a theory it had been lured into a pantechnicon-affair with a bunch of bananas.' Lord Canadine considered. 'Or perhaps of yams. I've no doubt you can buy yams at Fortnum's. But then they decided it had been a helicopter.'

'Might your statue have been removed by helicopter?'

'It's perfectly possible. On the other hand, a couple of strong men could have lugged it down the Gentlemen's Steps. Has Julia told you they're called that? Julia doesn't much care for this statue-business. She had no great fancy for my poor father, you know, and I don't altogether blame her. He was very much what you might call a smoking-room type. Wouldn't you say, Julia my dear?'

Lady Canadine's response to this was merely to give her distant kinswoman the ghost of a resigned glance. It seemed to combine an acknowledgement of the impropriety of her husband's talk with an indication that she herself was much too well-bred to take any open issue with it at the moment.

'Of course, when we opened up the house and gardens on a straight commercial basis, with no nonsense about local charities and so forth, we ought to have got this confounded indecent statue out of the way. I see that clearly enough now. But the fact is, it was a bit of a draw. *Plus ça change, plus c'est la même chose,* you might say. My father would stroll up here with two or three cronies after dinner, and the stupid thing would amuse them. And so with the trippers. Just the men, you know, as with those smutty little wall-paintings at Pompeii. I blame myself for not having put a stop to it. After all, it was Julia's duckweed that surrounded it, so permitting it wasn't really at all the thing.' Lord Canadine produced this sudden turn as a simple English gentleman without evincing any sign of self-consciousness. 'So that's the story of the statue, more or less. I think we ought to be getting back to the house for tea.'

There was nothing for it but her best behaviour, Judith told herself as, fifteen minutes later, she accepted a sandwich from her attentive host. Her visit hadn't been precisely an imposition, but she certainly wasn't entitled to assume the slightest degree of familiarity with the Canadines. She couldn't herself recur to the subject of the stolen statue in Lady Canadine's presence – not after having been told it was a theme Lady Canadine didn't care for. But Lord Canadine had seemed quite willing to be communicative, and this gave Judith an idea. Having continued to talk gardening over her first sandwich, she turned firmly to railways over her second. After all, it was no more than civil to show some awareness of this master-interest of her host's. The subject was not one to which Judith had addressed her mind for some time. Indeed, her only intimate acquaintance with it had been made in the schoolroom, or even the nursery, through the medium of a prized possession of her brother Mark called *The Wonder Book of Trains*. Her information, therefore, couldn't remotely be called up-to-date. But then a glimpse of the park at Netherway told one that its owner's interest in steam locomotion was organized on historical principles. Could Lord Canadine have possessed himself of George Stephenson's celebrated 'Rocket' – or still better of that steam road-carriage in which Nicholas Cugnot achieved, in the year 1770, a speed of three miles an hour – he would undoubtedly have given it pride of place in his collection. Judith, whose memory harboured such normally useless pieces of information as that the Trans-Siberian Railway was completed in the same year that the Panama Canal was begun, felt that it was ground upon which, at least for a brief period, she could put up a reasonable show. And Lord Canadine, suitably impressed, would offer to conduct her round his collection before she departed. Just this happened. Lord Canadine produced for Lady Appleby's acceptance a pictorial plan of his model railway system, and traced for her, with a well-manicured finger, the sundry gradients, embankments, and tunnels which he had constructed for it. Judith was so enchanted that, half an hour later, and after parting from Lady Canadine with sundry reciprocal undertakings as to the exchange of interesting roots and tubers, she found herself strolling through the park under convoy of her host. Scrambling in and out of the cabs of this vintage locomotive and that, she continued to keep her end up as well as she could. She ended by feeling far from certain that Lord Canadine wasn't amused. And this prompted her to a change of plan.

'How did you know,' she asked suddenly, 'that I was Lady Appleby?'

'I beg your pardon?' The tone of Lord Canadine's voice was politely uncomprehending.

'Your wife was speaking of a kinswoman, and introduced me simply as Judith Appleby. But you said "Lady Appleby" almost at once.'

'By jove, so I did! I remember it perfectly. Julia must have mentioned you on some previous occasion.'

'That isn't possible, I'm afraid. Lady Canadine had never heard of me.'

'You dropped in out of the blue?' This time, Canadine was more frankly amused. 'People do, of course. Men who are interested in locomotives, and women with a passion for duckweed. Perfectly natural. And one always welcomes a kinsman, of course.'

'You still haven't found an explanation.'

'My dear Lady Appleby, it's perfectly simple. As simple as my dear old friend, Archie Lyward. Lord Cockayne, that is. He tells me he's been trying to interest Sir John Appleby in a vanished picture. Clearly you were Lady Appleby, and interested in a vanished statue. There you were, questioning my wife about it.'

Judith climbed out of what she had been assured was a four-coupled express passenger engine designed by J. Holden for the Great Eastern Railway Company in 1904 (that inexhaustibly significant year: Trans-Siberian Railway, Panama Canal – and, for that matter, the publication by Mr Henry James of *The Golden Bowl*). At least she needn't climb into another of the things. For with Lord Canadine the moment of truth had arrived – a very fleeting moment of very minor truth, no doubt; but something, all the same.

'Yes,' Judith said. 'It's perfectly true. We're hot on a scent.'

'For a long time I've suspected it, in my dim and rural way.' Lord Canadine – who *was* a little mad, Judith fleetingly thought – laughed unaffectedly. 'I mean that, in this statue-affair, there was a shade more than met the eye. That, incidentally, went for the beastly thing itself. More met the eye than was decent. Or – shall we say? – than was grown-up. What's called a lavatory or prep-school humour, but done in stone. We needn't labour that.'

'Certainly we needn't, Lord Canadine. I know about it.'

'Well, I've wondered – or since I gathered the thing was valuable, I've wondered – whether that wasn't the nub of the matter. Pinch something its owner is reluctant to make a song about. Or pinch something in circumstances its owner doesn't feel quite free to ventilate. That's what applies to Archie's picture – although it was ever so long ago.'

'Archie?'

'Lord Cockayne.'

'Yes, of course. I forgot.' Judith was developing a considerable respect for the intelligence of Lord Cockayne's friend Lord Canadine. 'You mean you've wondered whether there may have been a series of such affairs?'

'Just that. And with Sir John and Lady Appleby both taking an interest in the matter, it does rather look as if my conjecture was confirmed. Would you care to look at any more of these toys of mine?'

'Not really.'

'I thought not. Has it occurred to you, by the way, that I must be very much my father's son? Boilers and bladders – the same sort of infantile interest in –'

'Quite. It's not a theme you need elaborate. Would you be upset, Lord Canadine, if the affair of your statue had to be publicized in the course of clearing up a series of such frauds and thefts?'

'Not in the least.' Canadine paused, as if surprised by what he had said. 'Odd, really – but one's feelings do change with the years, wouldn't you say? Perhaps it's simply that I feel Julia wouldn't be much upset now. Her mind is very much with the duckweed, just as mine is with these wretched steam-contraptions.' Lord Canadine, whose speech normally contrived a certain lightness of air, seemed for the moment to have struck a sombre note. 'We've both missed out on life, rather – Julia and I. No children, you know. And my business ought to have been with the public life of the country. What else is one a peer for – educated at those privileged places, and connected with all sorts of people more powerful than oneself? But I've done damn-all, and it's too late now.'

Judith said nothing. Perhaps Lord Canadine was hard-up for rational society – but he still ought not to have embarked on this sort of talk with a total stranger. He was a percipient character, all the same. And this emerged strikingly in what he said next.

'Lady Appleby – may I say that I greatly admire your work as a sculptor? And of course that's the real reason why I knew who you were! But doesn't it put you in a special relationship to what we're concerned with?'

'It certainly does. Your father's prank revolts me. But I didn't think I'd ever confess so much to anybody.'

'So we are friends, are we not?' Canadine's gaiety – for it was almost that – had returned. 'Can we be allies, too? Is there any way in which I can help this hunt?'

'You can tell me whether you have any idea how a thief came to know that the statue was valuable. You speak of the people who come to look at Netherway as trippers. Even if some of them got around to wandering up to that pool, it seems unlikely that among them would be somebody with an eye for valuable works of art in unexpected places.'

'Perfectly true. Or perfectly true, so far as the half a crown crowd is concerned.'

'The half a crown crowd?'

'That's our usual charge for both house and grounds. It's rather a moderate one – but, of course, Netherway isn't one of the major attractions in that line.'

'No elephants and camels.'

'Quite so. And nothing in the way of Titians and Velazquezes. But we do have a certain amount of fine furniture, which repays inspecting at leisure. So we run one Connoisseurs' Day a month – it's a common dodge – at ten bob. That does mean an occasional well-informed person prowling round.'

'I see. But there's another thing. You seem not to have known about the value of the statue yourself, and presumably your father didn't either. But somebody put you wise after the event, so to speak. That strikes me as rather odd. How did it come about?'

'I can certainly tell you about that. But it was an irritating business. I'd just as soon not have known the stolen statue had been of any value. I'd thought, you understand, that it had been lifted much as somebody might lift a china gnome or rabbit or toadstool from a suburban garden. Souveniring, as they say.'

'It would have been rather an unwieldy souvenir.'

'Perfectly true. But it seemed reasonable to suppose that it had been a theft motivated, at the most, by very petty gain, if not by mere whimsy. And then this fellow from Cambridge wrote to me. He'd heard of the disappearance, he said, from some common acquaintance of ours, and gathered I didn't know the thing was antique. So he'd felt I ought to be let know. Decent of him, wouldn't you say?'

'No doubt. But how did he come by any knowledge of the statue in the first place?'

'He was a Professor of Art, or something of the sort, and he'd been round Netherway with a group of distinguished foreigners. On a Connoisseurs' Day, I hope. He'd spotted the character of the statue at once, and been surprised to see such a thing simply standing about a garden, but he'd hesitated to make himself known to me and mention the matter – no doubt because of my father's treatment of the thing.'

'That seems reasonable enough. Who was this man?'

'He was called Sansbury. I remember the name, because I've come across it from time to time since. Quite a chap in his own line, I imagine. I never met him, you know. But I came to take his interest in my small misfortune quite kindly.'

'You mean you heard from Professor Sansbury more than once?'

'Oh, decidedly. We had quite a correspondence.'

'I find this a very strange business altogether.' Judith glanced curiously at her host. They were now approaching her car, and it was clear that in a few minutes she must depart. She wanted to leave as little as possible that was merely foggy behind her. 'What exactly was there to correspond about?' Judith paused. 'Perhaps he offered you an estimate of just *how* small your misfortune had been?'

'An estimate?' For the first time, Lord Canadine appeared a little put out. 'Well, yes. And, if he was right, it wasn't small, at all. The statue was quite surprisingly valuable. Indeed, as a poor man, I'd be inclined to say "fabulously". So it was all very irritating, as I've said. Still, it was amiable of this chap to go on being interested.'

'Just how did he go on?'

'Well, he thought it might be a good idea to find out about the statue's provenance. My father could have known no more about it than I did, but there might be a record of it somewhere in the family papers. Sansbury urged me to make a hunt. He'd be awfully interested, he said, to hear of anything. Odd, you think? It hasn't struck me that way before, but perhaps you're right. Learned chap, no doubt. That sort often likes collecting knowledge just for the hell of it. Scholarship, and so forth.'

For a moment, Judith said nothing. In his simpler vein, she somehow didn't find Lord Canadine altogether convincing. But she mustn't, she told herself, get imagining things. This sober resolution, however, was not very well answered by her next words.

'Did it occur to you,' she asked, 'that it might have been this Professor Sansbury who stole the statue?'

'My dear Lady Appleby, what an extraordinary idea!' Lord Canadine had paused by the door of Judith's car, and was staring at her in astonishment. 'If he was the thief, why in heaven's name should he deliberately bring himself to my notice? It doesn't make sense.'

'It *might* make sense. It might be some kind of bluff. And he was seeking information, wasn't he? If he was going to dispose of the thing on some sort of black market, it might be to his advantage to know something about its history. Suppose you had in fact hunted around, and found a record of a Canadine acquiring such a statue in, say, the mid-eighteenth century. You'd have let him know. And he'd have replied that the fact was extremely interesting from the point of view of a historian of art, and he'd be grateful if you'd lend him the document, or let him have a photographic copy of it. It would have enabled him to sell the statue to some clandestine collector, since he'd be holding virtual proof that it wasn't any sort of modern forgery.'

'But this Sansbury is obviously a most respectable character!' There was something like consternation in Lord Canadine's voice – as if before such suspicions as this one must feel the very bastions of society to be crumbling. 'Dash it all, Lady Appleby, Cambridge and all that, you know.'

'Perhaps I'm being fanciful. Such fantastic things used to come my husband's way, that I have a kind of domestic inclination in that direction.'

'Ah, yes – your husband. It would be a great pleasure to meet Sir John.' Lord Canadine frowned, as if feeling that he had given this too conventional an inflexion. 'I should like it very much. Might we make my unfortunate statue an excuse for a meeting? Or is he, by any chance, interested in railway engines? You really must both come over to lunch one day. Julia would be so pleased.' Lord Canadine had now opened the door of Judith's car. 'And how kind of you to have dropped in.'

'I did so enjoy seeing what Lady Canadine is doing.'

'Did you? But of course. The best duckweed in England.' Lord Canadine put out his hand. He was, after all, a peer of the realm, and accustomed to take such initiatives. 'It's best to turn right when you reach the village. Good-bye.'

Chapter Fourteen

The apartment in which Mr Praxiteles received Sir John Appleby had as its principal ornament a large El Greco of the most splendid sort. It was evident that to Mr Praxiteles the authenticity or otherwise of a lubricous painting by Giulio Romano would be a matter only of the most minor concern. The argosies of Mr Praxiteles sailed the seven seas; he was very well able to buy the Louvre or the Vatican if he took a fancy to it; his polite regard for his visitor alone seemed to prevent his declaring that the episode of Nanna and Pippa had been merely absurd and to be laughed at.

'I would venture to emphasize,' Appleby said, 'that you are not alone in being victimized. Others have been defrauded in related ways.'

'I am sorry to hear it, Sir John.' Mr Praxiteles extended in front of him two shapely and finely-tended hands. 'You recall La Rochefoucauld? *Nous avons tous assez de force pour supporter les maux d'autrui.* I have never concurred in so cynical a view. Every day, I am quite oppressed by the misfortunes I hear of as befalling total strangers. The philanthropic temper is a great misfortune, it seems to me. Reason, however, comes to one's aid. One can do nothing whatever about such calamities. One sighs, one even drops a tear, but one passes on.'

'I don't drop a tear, and I don't even sigh, Mr Praxiteles, over any of these frauds. There has been no robbing of widows and orphans –'

'That indeed would be distressing.'

'– and nobody is much worse off than he was before. But this has been going on for years – for a quite surprisingly long term of years – and it seems to me only common sense, and good citizenship too, to get rid of it. We owe some sort of duty to others who may be robbed in their turn.'

'How much I admire your sentiments, Sir John. It quite

pains me that I am unable to be of assistance to you. After all, it is the person Braunkopf who has been defrauded in this particular case.'

'May I say that it is nothing of the kind? It was *designed* that it should be Braunkopf who was defrauded, and so in fact it was for a time. But financially speaking, Braunkopf has retrieved his position at your expense. He has the real Giulio, and will sell it for quite as much as he believed he gave for it. You have the virtually worthless copy.'

'Yes, yes – of course.' Mr Praxiteles was indulgent rather than impatient. 'But what was this Giulio Romano? A not very proper picture, amusing to glance at now and then. And what is the copy? Just that. As I do not sell pictures, the matter of shillings and sixpences is quite indifferent to me. Have you a favourite charity, Sir John? I will give you a cheque for £12,000 for it this instant, and be wholly charmed. Such sums have no meaning for me. I hope I do not sound arrogant. It is the most detestable of vices, to my mind.'

'You mayn't sound arrogant, but you did look a fool. This fellow Braunkopf came along, had only to tell you that there might be humiliating publicity blowing up, and you obligingly handed over the real picture (which had been perfectly safely returned to you by whoever borrowed it for the purpose of swindling Braunkopf) in exchange for the worthless one. Doesn't the whole thing annoy you? Haven't you any impulse to fight back?'

'Ah, Sir John – now I must take issue with you. I fear you are adopting a posture – shall I say a stratagem? – not wholly to be approved by a person of unimpaired moral perception like myself. You are seeking to stir up malice and revenge in me, to play upon wounded vanity. Surely this is deplorable.'

For a moment Appleby said nothing – perhaps because what he would really have liked to do would be to kick this insufferable millionaire from one end to the other of his resplendent mansion. But that, of course, *would* be deplorable – and a great sensation in the newspapers tomorrow morning. Appleby tried another tack.

'I wonder,' he asked, 'whether you happen to know Lord Cockayne?'

'Cockayne? Yes, indeed. A delightful man. As it happens, he is after a seat on one of my boards. On the strength, I seem to recall, of one of his great-grandfathers having been an admiral. No doubt it is an adequate qualification, but unfortunately I have not yet been able to accommodate him. Lord Cockayne is perhaps a little past it, shall we say?'

'He is certainly an elderly man, and the first person I can trace as having been a victim of the series of frauds I am concerned with. Lord Cockayne is, of course, a person of consideration in English society.'

'But of course.' Mr Praxiteles was courteously acquiescent. 'Every Englishman loves a lord, does he not?'

'No doubt. But England has a great many lords.' Appleby paused impressively. 'And only one monarch.'

'I beg your pardon?' There was a fresh degree of attention in Mr Praxiteles' voice.

'Not that it is exactly a reigning monarch that was in question. Shall we say an August Personage, very close to the Throne?'

'My dear Sir John, I am at a loss to understand what you are talking about. Please enlighten me.'

'I am speaking of the first of these depredations – and, as I said, it was many years ago. There was an imposture, an impersonation. It involved an affront not merely to Lord Cockayne himself, but in the very highest circles. Quite properly, serious umbrage was taken at Court.'

'Dear me!'

'Lord Cockayne was persuaded to silence in the matter. A Special Messenger – I have no doubt he was a lord as well – was sent down to Keynes Court from one of the Royal Households. And the whole thing was hushed up.'

'Very properly, of course.' Quite suddenly, Mr Praxiteles was almost awed.

'But these things are not forgotten. A just resentment remains. And if the criminal author of this affront were brought quietly and discreetly to book, there would be corresponding gratitude, Mr Praxiteles, to all responsible. I think I may say that Grace and Favour would be shown in the most Exalted Quarter. You will not mistake me.' Appleby felt that he had not merely managed to cram, so to speak, a great many capital letters into this speech, but that he had virtually clapped the Royal Arms on top of it as well. 'And now I wonder,' he proceeded smoothly, 'how many of the circumstances connected with the disappearance of your picture are still within your recollection?'

'My memory is a very good one. Sir John. It is a faculty which the operations of ship-owning tend to strengthen. And I am, of course, charmed to help you in any way.'

But Mr Praxiteles, even when thus brought to a better mind, seemed not to have anything very useful to tell. That vanity had a fair share in his composition was clear enough; and vanity had persuaded him to make known to a good many people his proprietorship of an interesting cabinet of erotic paintings. He could be no means name everybody who had been conducted through it since its formation. He had been discreet, of course; not quite everybody appreciates that kind of thing; but there might have been occasions when some man familiarly known to him had dropped in accompanied by another man not known to him at all – and there had been a stroll through his little gallery without his having so much as noted the casual visitor's name. But he would not forget Sir John Appleby's, Mr Praxiteles urbanely added. And would Sir John care to make the little inspection now?

Appleby replied, perhaps a shade austerely, that nothing of the kind was necessary for his investigation, and that as a matter of pleasure it was something he would deny himself for the moment. He took it, on Mr Praxiteles's word, that pretty well anybody could have known of Mr Praxiteles's ownership of at least one painting which was fair game for the kind of operation under notice. And by 'fair game' was meant an artistic work of high monetary value, the subject of which made it probable that its owner would not make too public a fuss if somebody got monkeying around with it. Just this had happened to the Giulio; it had vanished, with some assurance that only a joke was involved, and that it would be returned again; fairly enough, it *had* been returned – and only the vigorous and unscrupulous action of the party whom it had actually been designed to defraud (Mr Braunkopf, to wit) was responsible for its not being snugly within its original proprietorship now. Mr Praxiteles – Appleby asked – would agree that this was a succinct statement of the matter? Mr Praxiteles agreed. So the main question, Appleby pursued, was how the picture had been borrowed, and how it had been restored again. He would be glad to hear what Mr Praxiteles had to say about this.

'There is no mystery about how the picture was returned to me. I received through the post a left-luggage ticket issued at Victoria Station. I went along there quietly in a taxi – it is as well to be unobtrusive about these things, is it not? – and collected the parcel which the ticket entitled me to. And my two dear girls – which is how I think of Nanna and Pippa, Sir John – were safe and sound inside it.'

'You made no attempt to engage the interest of the police in the matter?'

'None whatever. And there was assuredly no obligation upon me to do so. It was a mere joke that was being played upon me, was it not? English law is very odd about such things. A man can walk out of a public gallery with an important painting and hold on to it indefinitely – and yet, even if detected, it may be quite a business convicting him of theft. Isn't that strange?'

'I'm not sure, Mr Praxiteles, that you state the position quite accurately. In any case, it is not terribly relevant at the moment. I take it that, until Braunkopf turned up and virtually blackmailed you out of the returned picture in exchange for the copy, you had no inkling of his involvement in the affair?'

'None whatever. Of course, I have had dealings with the Da Vinci, as he calls his concern. But he didn't enter my head in connection with the disappearance of my girls.'

'I can see that there was no reason why he should.' Appleby paused. He felt a strong distaste for going back on his refusal to inspect Mr Praxiteles's little cabinet. But perhaps he would be obliged to, after all. 'About the copy now in your possession,' he said. 'Have you had it examined by an expert?'

'My dear Sir John, I *am* an expert. An able man – for let there be no false modesty between us – gets up these things, does he not? You want to know about the quality of the copy. But there is really little to say. It has been made by a skilled copyist, rather than by a practising artist, I think. But there are many such.'

'Are there many who would accept this particular sort of commission?'

'There was nothing out-of-the-way about the commission, surely?' Mr Praxiteles seemed surprised. 'The copyist could not know that the original he was to work from – or *she* was to work from, since many of these persons are ladies – had been purloined for the purpose.'

'It was a request for a rapidly executed copy of a highly improper painting by an Old Master.'

'A minor Old Master.' Mr Praxiteles was indulgent.

'No doubt. And you think there would be plenty of copyists to take on such a job, with no questions asked?'

'Dear me, yes. They are poor devils – the people who do such things. They seldom see a week's dinners securely in front of them, I should say.'

'It is a highly skilled copy? It seems to have taken in Braunkopf.'

'Yes – but only because he had seen the original, and received an authoritative expertise on it, only a few days before. He probably barely looked at the copy when it was delivered to him as the returned original. There lay the whole cleverness of the exercise, did it not?'

'Certainly it did. But the copy – the painting you now possess – is not to be described as a forgery?'

'Obviously not. You need only turn it face to the wall, and you will see that it can have been painted only the other day. The picture-surface itself is another matter. What they call the *craquelure* of the original had been reproduced. But Braunkopf could scarcely have been taken in even momentarily without that.'

'Now, perhaps, we are getting somewhere.' Appleby had sat up briskly. 'For isn't that outside an ordinary copyist's technique? Aren't these effects of shrinkage and movement, such as old pictures show, counterfeited only by electrical or chemical means?'

'I see you are informed about such matters, Sir John. It is only to be expected in a detective – you do not regard the term as derogatory? – of your eminence. The *craquelure* does introduce an element of forgery, no doubt. So does the particular varnish used. But there are, I imagine, plenty of people who could do the job.'

'Whoever did it required a canvas to do it on. The canvas might be traceable to a dealer, and a line on the copyist secured that way.'

'I think it improbable.'

'So do I. But one has to deal, you see, in possibilities as well as probabilities. And now, Mr Praxiteles, we come to the more important point. How was the picture stolen – or borrowed, if we are to prefer the term? I can't believe that you haven't considered the problem of security for your collection. Just how was it breached?'

'Most agreeably – from the point of view of a little light-hearted fun. And to give just *that* impression, of course, was valuable to the whole enterprise. You understand me, Sir John? Remove my poor girls in a fashion that would never enter a mere thief's head – in a fashion wholly bizarre, shall we say – and the presumption that it is a mere practical joke which is afoot becomes hard to resist.'

'Quite so. Let me say, Mr Praxiteles, that you are far from taking me to unfamiliar ground. Please go on.'

'Very well. The persons responsible for the rape of Nanna and Pippa – prepare to be staggered, my dear Sir John – were the President and Council of the Royal Academy.'

'I'm not staggered in the least. But I must confess I'm uncommonly interested.'

'I was in Paris at the time. I spend rather more of my time there than in London. Indeed, as you may see by glancing around you, I keep not much more than a camping-place here in England. In Paris I am less skimpily accommodated. I hope I may have the pleasure of receiving you there one day.'

'Thank you. It would be delightful. But please continue.'

'This little *pied-à-terre* was left in charge of my confidential man. He is a Cretan, by the way, which of course means that he is an incorrigible liar. Upon this occasion, nevertheless, I am convinced that he is speaking the sober – or the wildly inebriated – truth. He could not conceivably have invented the gentlemen from Burlington House. They turned up one morning in a couple of large cars. Their dress was exceedingly formal: silk hats, grey toppers, grey bowlers – all that sort of thing. Except that one of them was dressed like Lord Tennyson in the portraits, it seems: a flowing cloak and an enormous hat. That, no doubt, gave the authentic artistic touch. One of them presented what purported to be a note from me.'

'Authorizing them to make off with the Giulio?'

'It was a little more comprehensive than that. They were, in fact, a selection committee, and they were to take the pick of my collection for an exhibition of importance. The exhibition was to be opened – one of them mentioned casually – by the Archbishop of Canterbury.'

'The note was an effective forgery?'

'It is impossible to say, since my man was careless enough to throw it away afterwards. Or – more probably – he wanted to conceal how easily he had been taken in. Well, the President and his Council chose my delightful girls, removed them from the wall, and went away with them. It was as simple as that.'

'It was tolerably simple, certainly, granted the near-imbecility of your servant. They must have banked on that.'

'No doubt means were taken to explore his degree of credulity. And perhaps I was at fault in employing him. But a fellow who is not too sharp-witted has his convenience at times. You must have experienced that.'

'I can't say that I have.' Appleby spoke without much cordiality.

'And yet I must put in a good word for Aleko. He at least remembered that he ought always to ask for a name. He had some dim apprehension of the significance of the office –'

'President of the Royal Academy?'

'Yes. But Aleko felt that he ought to have the gentleman's actual name as well. So he asked for it, quite firmly, as these fellows were making off with their booty. And the President gave his name without hesitation. It turned out to be Sir Joshua Reynolds. Aleko wrote it down – or wrote down a rough phonetic equivalent of it – as soon as his visitors had departed.'

'Do you think that Aleko had ever heard the name of Joshua Reynolds?'

'It is most improbable.' Mr Praxiteles made a slight gesture across the room. 'He has heard of El Greco.'

'He might have been none the better off if he *had* heard of Reynolds. It is a subject upon which a little knowledge appears to be a dangerous thing.'

'I do not quite understand you, Sir John.'

'A mere idle thought. No doubt this absurdity about Reynolds added to your sense of assurance that the whole thing was a mere joke?'

'Certainly it did. As did the little reference to the Archbishop of Canterbury. One has to smile – would you not say, Sir John? – at the thought of his Grace unveiling, as it were, my dear girls.'

'It is certainly not a service they stand in need of. By the way, just what means did these people take to tell you that you would get your picture back?'

'The leader – shall we call him Sir Joshua? – simply left a sealed note for me in Aleko's hands. It was typewritten, as you may imagine.'

'And it said?'

'What it said, Sir John, I can quote from memory. *The Secretary of the Society begs to inform Mr Praxiteles that his picture,* Nanna and Pippa, *has been borrowed for the purpose of exhibition at the Society's annual banquet. It will be returned to Mr Praxiteles immediately thereafter.*'

'I see. But just what was this Society? It didn't purport to be the Royal Academy?'

'Ah, no. The joke was being taken a little further. The letterhead was that of the Society for the Suppression of Vice.'

Chapter Fifteen

'Daddy not down yet?' said Bobby Appleby, and surveyed the breakfast table with a critical and expectant eye. 'Hoobin is annoying Mrs Colpoys by sitting in her kitchen waiting instructions to begin weeding the drive or something. And until the oracle speaks, Hoobin will sit.'

'Then Hoobin must be indulged.' Judith Appleby poured coffee. 'I'm certainly not going to disturb your father. He arrived home very late.'

'Well, well! The shocking old roisterer.'

'I don't think he's been madly gay. He went up to London again, when he heard he could see the man Praxiteles.'

'The owner of Guilio Romano's naughty wenches?'

'Yes. He rang up afterwards and said he'd only catch the last train, because he had a number of arrangements to make.'

'You mean he turned mysterious? Would you call that a good sign?'

'I suppose he didn't want to say too much on the telephone. I rather gathered that he wasn't coming straight back from town, but was just dashing off somewhere else.'

'Not to Keynes, I hope.' Bobby helped himself to what had some appearance of being both his own and his father's bacon and sausages. 'That's something I want to be in on with him. As a matter of fact, I thought he might drive me over today, and drop me in Oxford on his way home. I oughtn't to be away from the old place too long. It's wonderful how they miss me.' Bobby, although only beginning on his first sausage, took a prospective glance inside the marmalade pot. 'When I got back to college after my last little excursion, my tutor stopped me in the quad and said how particularly delighted he was to see me in residence again. Nice of him, don't you think?' Bobby picked up *The Times*, assured himself at a glance that its interest for him was nil, and obligingly laid it beside his father's place at table. 'Do you think,' he asked, 'that the deep Sir John Appleby has a plan?'

'I'm almost sure he has, but I've no idea what it is.'

'He'll have to tell us. This is turning into quite a family affair, wouldn't you say? We'll have to swap information as soon as he appears.'

'Here he is.'

'So there we are,' Bobby said, half an hour later. 'Mummy and I have pretty well done the job for you, it seems to me. But we'd still better go to Keynes, since Oswyn's old dad expects you. And then I must get back to Oxford, no doubt. But your real goal is Cambridge.'

'Cambridge, my dear lad? You think it would be useful to pay a visit to Cambridge?' Appleby helped himself to what remained in the coffee-pot. 'And you can tell me what to do when I get there?'

'Get the local dicks to arrest this shocking Professor Sansbury, I suppose. It's him, isn't it? The thing that sticks out a mile. It was Sansbury who authenticated the Giulio for Braunkopf –'

'I'm not altogether clear how that ties up with the notion that he had also done the borrowing of it.'

'It amused him to play a double role, so to speak. One in Braunkopf's shop under his own name, and one *chez* Praxiteles, under the name of Sir Joshua Reynolds P.R.A.' Bobby paused to light his pipe. 'And I've discovered for you that it was Sansbury who valued Carrington's pictures, and actually wanted to carry off the Stubbs on the pretext of having it cleaned. That's about enough in itself. But now Mummy has found it was Sansbury who wrote and told Lord Canadine about the value of his statue –'

'Wasn't that a rum thing to do, if it was he who had already pinched it?'

'He wanted Canadine to dig up information about its provenance. And he was just being freakish. *That* fits in, surely. The freakish is what turns up in this business every time.'

'I certainly agree with you there. But just what have we got?

This man Sansbury – who doesn't, by the way, strike me as all that freakish – bobs up in one or another relationship to three of these affairs. Are we to call that statistically significant?'

'Of course we are.'

'Suppose that there have been a good many more of these frauds and thefts and impostures than we have yet tabs on – which seems to me a probability in itself. Suppose that we did come on half a dozen others, and that Sansbury seemed unconnected with any of them. It would then simply be a matter of coincidence that we had come early upon the three he does figure in. Well, why *shouldn't* he figure – quite innocently and harmlessly – in three out of nine such episodes? His professional world, after all, must be an uncommonly small one.'

'I wonder,' Judith said, 'whether Professor Sansbury of Cambridge lives in what can be called at all a big way? There has been very considerable money in these operations – even if there have *not* been more in the series than we are aware of. And dons live much of a muchness, so far as economic level goes. If they don't, all their acquaintance knows just why. One man has always been understood to possess inherited wealth, and another is recalled as having married money. That sort of thing.'

'But dons can obviously have the most luscious secret lives.' Bobby offered this contribution to the debate with confidence. 'The humblest of them, donkeying away as college tutors and so on, need be around for just twenty-four weeks in the year. And professors and people are like our Master, and other heads of colleges. If they care to, they can be completely invisible from year's end to year's end. Living it up like anything, in haunts of idleness and sin.'

'I hope,' Appleby said, 'you will not so indulge your flair for facile exaggeration when you come to write those papers in your Final Honour School. There is, nevertheless, something in what you say. It would not clear Sansbury of suspicion simply to show that, when in Cambridge, he doesn't fling money about. Nor would it clear him if we found another and stronger suspect.'

'Because there must be a gang?'

'Well, something approximating to a gang. There are two very prominent features in the affair, you know. The first is that there has been continuous, or at least intermittent, operation over quite a long period of years. And the second is that some, at least, of the operations have involved considerable team-work.'

'Or at least,' Judith said, 'the employment of supers. Take the Praxiteles incident. Apart from Sansbury himself, who turns up in it only at the Da Vinci and merely in an ambiguous and possibly innocent way, there need only have been one person capable of sustaining more than a walking-on role. It was Sir Joshua Reynolds who did the talking to Praxiteles's man Aleko, and who enjoyed little private jokes like the one about the Archbishop of Canterbury. The others had merely to look like moderately important persons. Like people hired by movie-directors to do background dining and wining in expensive restaurants. I've sometimes wondered whether real food and drink is provided.'

'I think there's a third prominent feature,' Bobby said. 'The whole series of frauds avoids anything that could be called the darker face of crime. Nobody has really been frightfully hurt.'

'Just that has been in my head more than once.' Appleby paused, frowning. 'And it ought, in a way, to be reassuring. We are hunting for some very clever, but rather harmless, rogue. But one oughtn't to be too careless. In terms of fortune on the one hand, and legal penalty on the other, the stakes are fairly high.' Appleby stood up. 'I think Bobby and I ought to be moving. Keynes Court, then Oxford, and then Cambridge suggests rather a long day.'

'You *will* go to Cambridge?' There was astonishment in Bobby's voice.

'But of course. Professor Sansbury must at least be invited to explain himself.'

'Then, couldn't you make it Keynes Court, Cambridge, and Oxford? I'd rather like to be –'

'Definitely not, Bobby. I drop you in college, and drive on.'

'As you please, of course.' Bobby Appleby was annoyed. 'But if you really feel that I shall be failing to keep up with their simple academic exercises merely because I'm not in lecture-rooms for an odd –'

'Absolutely nothing of the kind.' Appleby turned quickly to his son. 'You can be off to Kamchatka, if you please, and it won't affect my guess that you'll be all right on the day. It's simply that I don't want to arrive in Cambridge accompanied by an Oxford undergraduate son. Is that obscure?'

'It's not exactly luminous,' Judith said. She was stacking cups and saucers on a trolley. 'But I do see a glimmer. Has it something to do with not being careless?'

'Yes, it has. Bobby, did you tell that chap Carrington a lot about yourself?'

'I don't know that I'm all that the adolescent egocentric.' This time, Bobby was not offended. 'But I didn't have a chance, really. He knew a good deal about me already – Rugger-wise, you understand.'

'Yes, of course. Fame has its penalties. Judith, what about the Canadines? Did you tell them all about the present doings of our young?'

'While exhibiting the family snapshots? I didn't, as a matter of fact. It was pretty well alpines and aquatics all the time.' Judith pushed the trolley soothingly towards Mrs Colpoys, who had appeared with the obvious intention of making stiff representations about the inertia of the aged Hoobin. 'And now, do go away, both of you. I have quite a long day's work, too.'

Bobby rather enjoyed being driven by his father in the solid and by no means pristine Rover. The vehicle, too, was very much a family affair; one felt there ought to be a scramble of children in the back and a picnic-basket tucked away behind. With his father at the wheel, one didn't exactly drink the wind of one's own speed; on the other hand their progress wasn't an irritating dawdle. It was reasonable to suppose that, when younger, Sir John Appleby (Inspector Appleby, as he had no doubt been called) had driven faster – as fast as Bobby Appleby (Scrum-half Appleby, one might say) was prone to do. Bobby wondered whether his father had solved mysteries faster, as well. But of course one had to remember that the business on hand was not just one mystery but a whole little crop of them, and that the first (which was the one they were after now) dated from a time when Oswyn Lyward – a person whose notable maturity of manner impressed Bobby very much – had been more or less biting his own toes in his modestly coroneted cradle. Oswyn's father – Bobby's father had divulged with delight – was in the expectation that the perplexed episode of the spurious royal visit was now to be briskly solved by a quick hunt for finger-prints. These would have to leap – Bobby told himself with the poet – from hiding-places ten years deep. Or rather twenty years deep. And so would any other clues which Keynes Court was likely to harbour. So it would be naïve to expect, with Lord Cockayne, really quick results.

Bobby glanced sideways at his father, and received a strong impression of great concentration. It was possible, of course, that his father had merely assumed the expression proper in an elder-ly man when driving a staid 3-litre Rover along an empty coun-try road. On the other hand, perhaps the mystery was being sorted out. So Bobby forbore to converse.

'Did you bring *The Times*?' Appleby asked suddenly.

'Yes. You told me to.'

'Then read out the clues.'

'The clues?' For a moment, Bobby was bewildered. Then he said 'All right,' resignedly, and turned to the back page.

'Look at your watch,' Appleby said. 'No fun without that. Begin.'

'*Tutor has a crib, the hearing is lengthy. Six.*'

'There's usually an easy start,' Appleby said, and braked carefully before a corner. '*Donkey.*'

'Of course.' Bobby sighed, and fished for a pencil. 'Begins with *D. Army arithmetic. Eight.*'

'*Division.*' Appleby had been obliged to think for a moment. 'We'll speed up soon.'

'I suppose so,' Bobby said, and let his eye stray to a mile-stone. 'Here's one I can do at once. *Pater's art? Four.* That's Dada.'

'Ought to be Gaga,' Appleby said cheerfully. 'Carry on.'

'I suppose,' Bobby said half an hour later, and when the puzzle had been completed, 'that that's what you call resting your mind.'

'Why should I rest my mind? It's not in a state of conval-escence.' Appleby laughed. 'Or why shouldn't I, for that mat-ter? Ought it to be obsessed with something?'

'Of course it should. With this sleuthing we're busying over. With the mystery.'

'Oh, I wouldn't say there was a mystery, you know. Is that Keynes across the valley?'

'Yes, it is. Terrific, isn't it? Not so much a country seat as a country sofa. What do you mean that there isn't a mystery?'

'I mean that the chain of events is all pretty clear. But one link is likely to be bogus. Have you thought of that? Find a bogus link, and the whole thing is tied up. Not, of course, that there isn't a real snag. We have to reckon on submerged links, so to speak. We were noting that at breakfast. There may well have been a number of other operations during the long period of years since the Keynes Court one. They just haven't come our way. They are on the record, as being known to the parties immediately concerned, but they're not on the police record. The bogus link may be one of these submerged ones. It's not a probability, but it's a possibility. Do we go over the bridge?'

'Yes. It was built by Oswyn's great-grandpapa. I don't understand this about a bogus link. Explain.'

'I don't say that its existence is a certainty, by any means. But put it like this, Bobby. Suppose you are planning for yourself not just a single highly remunerative crime, but a long sequence of highly remunerative crimes. What sort of person are you likely to be?'

'An optimist, I suppose. The more crimes you carry out, the more likely you are to get nabbed in the end. Of course, it depends on the sort of crime. We're confining ourselves to this picture-pilfering business and the like, I suppose.'

'Yes, of course. And you certainly have to reckon on an increasing chance of being nabbed in the end, as you say. But you also have to reckon on *suspicion*. As the operations go on, there is bound to be a hunt for the operator. The police may eventually establish a category of suspected persons. What's the best way of ensuring that you won't find yourself in it?'

'I see. It's an easy one. Get yourself fixed up in the *other* category – that of the victims. Which is what you mean by a bogus link. How simple these things are, when one gives one's mind to them.'

'Most sham robberies and so forth are insurance rackets.

The kind I'm thinking of would be an insurance racket of a special sort.' Appleby had slowed to a decorous thirty miles an hour. 'This seems to be the sort of park that has whole villages tucked away in corners of it.'

'In about half a mile you cross the river by an Irish bridge –'

'Whatever is that?'

'It's just a bridge, but built under the water instead of over it.'

'Extremely sensible.'

'So it's really a reliable sort of ford, and supposed to be picturesque. A bit after that, you go over a cattle-grid, and are in the deer park. And then you run along the side of the lake and come to the house. All the gardens are on the other side.'

'Not very populous is it?' Appleby said as they splashed over the Irish bridge. 'The peasants cower in their hovels until summoned to perform their corvé for their feudal lord. And I don't see any deer either.' The Rover had rattled over the cattle-grid. 'But one has to admire the trees.'

'Somebody coming now,' Bobby said. 'But not a plodding hind.'

'A wanderer from the great house, I think, out for a meditative stroll.'

This was evidently correct; the figure they were about to pass on the drive was very much that of a gentleman at leisure.

'I don't think it's a member of the family,' Bobby said. 'But shall we give him a wave? Perhaps it's –'

'Bobby – *duck*!'

It was probably the memories of Cowboys and Indians played with his parents and brothers long ago that was responsible for Bobby Appleby's obeying this startling injunction instantly. He vanished beneath the dashboard rather as if he had been ignominiously engulfed by one of his own scrums. Once there, he doubtless expected some dramatic development – perhaps the crack of a pistol-shot in the near vicinity. But nothing of the kind occurred, and after two or three hundred yards the car came to a stop.

'All right,' Appleby said.

'Just what was that in aid of, please?' As he dusted himself down, Bobby allowed himself a very natural indignation.

'You can think it out as you go on your way. It will do instead of another crossword puzzle.'

'What do you mean – on my way?'

'On your way to Oxford, my dear boy. I suppose you're capable of getting out of this park without being seen?'

'I suppose so, if I try.'

'Then try quite hard, and oblige your ageing parent.' Appleby chuckled. 'Bobby, I'm terribly sorry. But clear out.'

'Oh, very well.' Bobby, who could be almost alarmingly a paragon of filial duty, grinned cheerfully, and clambered from the car. 'The Lywards had their own private railway station, but I believe it has been closed down. However, there's a nice little market town not much more than twenty miles away. Just right for stretching one's legs. And it's rather flattering to have become a dark secret. Or am I the family skeleton?'

'Neither the one nor the other, I'm afraid. You're just my youngest son, and currently up at Oxford. By the way, will your friend Oswyn Lyward be at Keynes now?'

'I don't think so. He's terribly tied up with some essays.'

'Good. Do you think his father is likely to recall your existence, without Oswyn there to jog his memory?'

'Most improbable, I'm afraid. Well, the unmentionable Appleby Junior vanishes. Over hill, over dale, thorough bush, thorough brier.'

'Over park, over pale, thorough flood, thorough fire. I hope it won't come quite to that. By the way, have you enough money?'

'Plenty, thanks.' Bobby was amused by this agreeable paternal solicitude. 'I say, can I have one guess at who that chap was we passed?'

'One guess is fair enough.'

'Your Cambridge friend, Professor Sansbury.'

'You get a clear alpha on that,' Appleby said. And he let in the clutch and drove on.

Part Three

The Trap

Chapter Sixteen

'Most kind of you to come down,' Lord Cockayne said politely. Perhaps out of absence of mind, or perhaps by way of lending force to his words, he shook hands with Appleby a second time. He had received his visitor in a sombrely panelled great hall, hung with darkened family portraits to which only a greenish and subaqueous light penetrated through heavily mullioned windows. This milieu its proprietor had evidently thought to enliven by importing sundry memorials of his own life and career. The Indian carpet had certainly been woven in the gaols of Agra. On each side of the chimney piece – and flanking Lord Cockayne now – stood a stuffed Bengal tiger. The effect would have been strikingly heraldic but for the fact that the creatures' architectural surroundings reduced them to the proportions of those twinned china dogs which doubtless occupied a corresponding position by the hearths of many of Lord Cockayne's humbler tenants.

'Delighted to have your expert help,' Lord Cockayne said. 'I expect you've brought your plan?'

'I certainly have something in mind.' Appleby looked at his host in some surprise.

'Well, we must go and have a look. But I ought to tell you that there are bats. You don't mind bats?'

'Not in the least.'

'Capital, my dear sir, capital. And they're where one ought to expect them, after all. Bats in the belfry, eh? Ha-ha!' Lord Cockayne set out on a somewhat wandering course across the vast Jacobean hall. 'I don't want to hurry you – in India I made a point of never hurrying anyone, and it was a policy that was very well received – but, of course, we shall require the thing in time for the actual anniversary. They'll want to fool around with it on the occasion.'

'The anniversary?'

'Ah, I see you haven't been told. Well, I've been looking into my family history, of which there is really a surprising amount, and I can't find any record of the thing having happened before. To a son here or a brother there, maybe. But never to a holder of the title. So I felt, you know, that it had to be thought about. The tenantry will come along with goodness knows what, and there ought to be a *quid pro quo* for the village. I ran through all the commonplace things: cricket pavillion, new hall for the Women's Institute, swings and so forth for the children. And then this came to me. You don't mind a short walk through the park?'

'Not in the least. But you mean that there came to you, by way of celebrating some anniversary, the notion of presenting the village with a picture – a *missing* picture, which may be very valuable, or may be worth nothing at all?'

'Picture? Nothing of the kind. What would a picture have to do with my golden wedding? This bell for the church, of course. Come this way.'

'I'm afraid,' Appleby said, 'that there is some misapprehension.'

'Misapprehension? Nonsense! If *you* had been married for fifty years, my dear sir, you wouldn't be in any misapprehension about it.'

'I hope the bell will be a great success. But I have nothing whatever to do with it.'

'Nothing to do with it! Do you mean to assert that you are not the fellow recommended to me by the Campanological Society?'

'The only bells I know much about are in police cars and fire engines and ambulances.'

'God bless my soul!'

'My name is Appleby, and I've come down to Keynes at your invitation, Lord Cockayne, to look into the matter of a missing picture. A picture missing for a long time.'

'Perfectly right. I've been feeling for months that something ought to be done about it.' Lord Cockayne thus changed gear without a trace of discomfiture. 'And, of course, we knew that you were the man, my dear Sir John. My youngest boy – I wonder whether you know Oswyn? – was quite clear that you were the man. If a person of your eminence could at all be interested in the matter, that is to say. And here you are. Most delightful. I hope you can stay to lunch? Or till the end of the month? I'm very sorry my wife's away from home. Gone to visit a former housekeeper of ours in Cheltenham. We got her turned into a Distressed Gentlewoman. One must be a shade unscrupulous, these days. Not that I don't recall her as a very civil-spoken person. Now, where would you say we ought to begin? I am entirely at your command – my dear Appleby, if I may so address you. Except that I am expecting a man about a bell. Tell you about that over luncheon. Ties up with having been married the devil of a long time. Would you care to see where the picture hung?'

The picture had hung in the Long Gallery. This was a magnificent specimen of its kind, running the full length of the main façade of Keynes Court. In contrast with the gloomy hall below, it gave an impression of being filled with light – partly because it broadened several times into room-like bays with enormous windows, and partly because its moulded ceiling and elaborately panelled walls had been painted white and enriched with gilding. But these decorations appeared to have been achieved a long time ago, for the paint had taken on a yellow tinge and the gilding was in places flaking away.

'Sense of elbow room up here,' Lord Cockayne was saying. 'Not much used, however, since the children grew up. All sorts of games in wet weather: badminton, skittles, even archery. So quite a sensible place, really. One's surprised that people don't build more of them. Got one yourself?'

'Well, yes – but nothing near a quarter as long, I'd say.'

'Ah.' Lord Cockayne was sympathetic. 'All right for draughts and dominoes, eh? The picture hung there, my dear fellow. Haven't put anything in its place, as yet, although I've been meaning to for some little time. Miss it, rather.'

Appleby looked at the blank space on the wall. It didn't seem too informative – but then he had scarcely expected it to be.

'You miss it?' he said. 'You'd recognize it, if you saw it again?'

'Recognize it?' It could only be said that Lord Cockayne stared. 'Why, it's one of my favourite things up here. Tell you the truth, I was most devilishly annoyed when my exalted visitor showed she had a mind to it.'

'But she wasn't an exalted visitor at all – only somebody dressed up as one.'

'That's right.' Lord Cockayne seemed just to have recalled this fact, and to be prepared to regard it as an exacerbating circumstance. But then his mind wandered again. 'I've always insisted, you know, that they're very decent people in their way. Take George the Third. Shockingly maligned, but a thoroughly nice chap. Bit of a statesman, too. Managed to lose us the Americans – ha ha!'

Appleby echoed 'ha ha!' rather absent-mindedly. He was reflecting that almost his only information about the Keynes Court affair came from Oswyn Lyward, and that Oswyn's account had been influenced to an unknown degree by the need to sustain before his fellow Patriarchs a cherished reputation as a raconteur. He was diverted, however, from pursuing the implications of this further by observing a fresh oddity in the behaviour of his host. Lord Cockayne was sniffing the air of his Long Gallery as a man might do who thinks that something has gone wrong with the gas.

'At least the paint has stopped smelling,' Lord Cockayne said.

'The paint?'

'It was one of the awkward things about that bally royal visit –'

'That bogus royal visit.'

'So it was.' Lord Cockayne nodded sagely. 'We were doing some decorating in rather a big way, as you can see.' He waved comprehensively at his surroundings. 'All this white paint, for example. And it's not a smell that such people are used to, eh? Did I tell you that there was something odd about her voice?'

'The august visitor's?'

'Yes. We thought she had a bad cold, but she may have been what's-its-name to paint.'

'Allergic?'

'That's it. New-fangled word, but my own mother suffered

from the thing. Riding to hounds would bring her out in spots. Tragic, eh? And she didn't stay long.'

'Your mother?'

'No, no – this royal impostor. Nobbled my Madonna, and off she went.'

'I see.' Appleby reflected that there were at least substantial correspondences between Lord Cockayne's uncertain recollections and Lord Oswyn Lyward's not wholly reliable narrative. 'What sort of a Madonna was it?'

'Very attractive. Good, broad hips. In fact, nearly all hips. Capital for child-bearing, you know. Obviously the Holy Ghost –' Lord Cockayne checked himself. 'The children called her the Wedge. She was rather that shape.'

'She sounds like an Italian Primitive.'

'That's right. I don't know that I've ever mentioned it to anybody, or that it has so much as come up into my head since. But some long-haired chap brought down here by my wife once told me he thought he could put a name to the painter. Duccio. Ever heard of him? Operated before the real nobs, of course.'

Such is the irrational influence of great names that Appleby found himself looking with momentary awe at the small blank space on the wall in front of him. *Duccio di Buoninsegna, first and greatest of the Sienese, hung here.* Or so some long-haired chap had thought.

'Can you recall,' Appleby asked, 'the name of the man who suggested to you that the painting might be by Duccio?'

'Lord, no!' Lord Cockayne appeared surprised. 'All sorts of people come around, you know. Tiresome having to be civil to them sometimes. Duty, all the same.'

'Yes.' Appleby reflected that he himself was receiving civility. 'Is there anybody else who might know?'

'I hardly think so. But – yes, by Jove! – young Sansbury might. And he's here for the week-end.'

'I know Professor Sansbury, and I saw him in your park. A long-haired chap himself, isn't he?'

'Ah, yes.' Lord Cockayne glanced with momentary suspicion at Appleby. 'But he's an old friend, as a matter of fact. Been around Keynes from time to time ever since he was a kid. Lord knows who the Sansburys were. But his mother was a

Southdown.' Lord Cockayne paused. 'Never gone in for snob-bery,' he said. 'Set my face against it in India. Raised difficulties sometimes. But not the right thing in old families.'

'I've no doubt you're right.' Appleby spoke inattentively; he was suddenly looking yet more seriously at the wall in front of him. 'Lord Oswyn,' he said, '– who was good enough to introduce me to you, you know – has told me the story of the picture's disappearance. But, of course, he was much too young to be present. He speaks from hearsay, and may have got things a little wrong. He says that you yourself took the picture from the wall, blew some dust off it, rather to the annoyance of Lady Cockayne –'

'Oswyn says that? Absolute nonsense! How could there be dust on the thing, with this whole gallery still sticky with new paint?'

'It does seem a point. Oswyn then says that a well-drilled equerry took two steps forward, received the picture from you, and took two steps back. He was accustomed to the whole manoeuvre, that is to say. And then the visit ended. Would you say that's right?'

'Nothing of the kind, my dear fellow. I'd have been less off-ended if it had been. And – do you know? – looking back on the affair, I can see it was a point at which these impostors slipped up. I can't think why I didn't spot it at the time. What happened was that, the moment I'd said what pleasure it would give me if my visitor would accept the thing, this court functionary, or equerry as you call him, stepped forward and took the picture from its hook himself. Incredible, once you think of it. Too damned bad form for these – Too damned bad form, I mean. I was deuced glad the bally bounder messed himself up.'

'Perhaps you mean –?' Appleby had advanced closer to the wall.

'The white paint, or enamel, or whatever it is. It was what they call tacky, you know.' Lord Cockayne paused – and then added with his intermittent vagueness, 'Of course, it's dry now, as you can see.'

'I can see more than that.' Appleby was staring almost in-credulously at the ancient paint-work before him. 'He put a finger on the stuff, and the print's there still.'

'Most interesting to have met here,' Professor Sansbury said. He and Appleby were alone together after lunch. For the person recommended by the Campanological Society had now really arrived, and Lord Cockayne had withdrawn to confer with him.

'Yes, indeed,' Appleby said. 'I had no idea you were a friend of the Lywards.'

'I don't quite know why you should.' Sansbury had raised his eyebrows. 'It was only the other day that you and I met for the first time, after all.'

'Very true. A casual introduction in a club smoking-room. But we did fall into a certain amount of talk about missing pictures. And I mentioned my interest in one that had vanished from Keynes Court.'

'So you did. It had quite escaped me.' Sansbury spoke without any appearance of concern. 'I had rather forgotten, I'm afraid. It was naturally the Braunkopf affair – which had a good deal worried me, you recall – that was in my mind. Oddly enough, Cockayne has never mentioned his own loss to me. The circumstances, so far as I gathered them at lunch, seem to have been exceedingly odd. But it was all a long time ago, was it not?'

'Certainly it was. But not, I believe, before you were in the habit of visiting at Keynes. Lord Cockayne even believes you may remember something important from that time. A casual guest told him that the picture we are now concerned with might be by Duccio. Cockayne thinks you might remember who that person was.'

'I know nothing whatever about it, I'm afraid.'

'And you don't recall ever having taken note of the picture yourself? There it was, after all, in the Long Gallery. And the history of art was already your profession, I suppose.'

'Of course. But I doubt whether I was ever so much as shown the Long Gallery in those days. Cockayne has perhaps exaggerated the extent of my intimacy with his family. It has been quite occasional. The old gentleman is apt, you must have noticed, to get things a little distorted. Particularly the passing of time.'

'That is true. But, talking of oddity, I'm rather struck, Professor, by the fact that your having a long-standing, even if intermittent, acquaintance with Keynes didn't turn up in our first conversation. The run of our talk, I seem to recall, would have made it natural.'

'May I speak of oddity too, Sir John?' With fingers which Appleby thought were not wholly steady, Sansbury was stuffing a pipe. 'To be quite frank, there is something more than a little odd in the way you are presuming to question me. I hope I don't offend you.'

Appleby took his time about meeting this challenge. He was not sure that Sansbury had done well to offer it. Sansbury was a person of some eminence in his particular walk of life. One was inclined to assume that he was a very clever man, and it was certain that he couldn't be a fool – or not in the sense of being slow-witted or stupid. He could hold his own, clearly enough, in any sort of sophisticated conversation. That was what he had been doing when Appleby first became aware of him – putting up lively academic chit-chat with no less a personage than the Astronomer Royal. But was he, for example, conceited in a haz-ardous fashion? Was he a man who, somehow, had been carried a little – or a lot – out of his depth? Quite a short time – Appleby told himself – was now going to show. Meanwhile, the best pol-icy was attack – but attack pressed not quite home.

'You must forgive my curiosity,' he said urbanely. 'One of my interests – an old professional interest, you will understand – is what may be called the limits of coincidence. How thick on the ground must coincidences be before one is obliged to admit that something *not* coincidental is involved? I don't presume to ask myself this in terms of the theory of probability. I'm neither a mathematician nor a philosopher, but just a plain retired policeman. Can I give you a match?'

It was true that Professor Sansbury was making rather an ineffective business of lighting his pipe. Appleby paused long enough to allow ample time for the operation, and then went on.

'And you are, if I may say so, a most interesting case in point. I'm not unaware – indeed, I was remarking on it to somebody the other day – that yours must be quite a small world. Smaller, say, than my own, or than that of the professional criminal. So, in matters relating to your calling, my dear Professor, it would be quite natural to find your name – a most distinguished name – bobbing up quite a lot. That's certainly what I've been finding.'

'You really talk in riddles, Sir John. A trick of the trade, no doubt.'

'I think you know Sir Thomas Carrington?'

'Carrington? Sir *Thomas* Carrington? The name does seem to ring a bell.'

'The name ringing a bell is that of a gentleman who was ingeniously robbed of a picture by George Stubbs.'

'I'm very sorry to hear it.' Sansbury's smile might have been intended as urbane, but in fact rendered a slightly strained effect. 'Why ingeniously, Sir John?'

'I suspect that the Stubbs could have been stolen in a much more straightforward fashion. The ingenuity seems to have been partly the consequence of a perverted sense of fun – an impulse to do things the play-way, as it were. But it was partly a matter of making Carrington feel ridiculous, and so indisposed to create a fuss.'

'How very curious. And now I do recollect. I valued the man's pictures. A routine job, not leaving much mark on the mind.'

'Did coming on a Stubbs leave no mark on your mind? At the time, at least, you were sufficiently interested to offer to take the picture away and have it cleaned.'

'An obvious civility. Yes, the incident does come back to me.'

'Does your correspondence with Lord Canadine come back to you?'

'Good Lord, yes! The affair of the outraged statue. Who could forget a thing like that? When I heard that it had gone, I thought I ought to write to him, letting him know how valuable it was. He hadn't a clue, and it seemed a plain public duty. Of course I ought to have let him know – or found out whether he *did* know – the moment I saw the thing so vulnerably disposed in his garden. But it would have been awkward, in view of the indelicate manner in which it had been treated.'

'I see. But I think I'm right in saying that, once you had, so to speak, broken the ice, you *continued* to correspond with Canadine?'

'I did, indeed. I wanted to discover where the stolen statue had come from, and so forth. Its story would have a distinct place in the history of taste.'

There was now a pause in this curious catechism. Sansbury was being told nothing that it had been particularly difficult to find out – yet what he was dissimulating was quite as much surprise as alarm. He had remarked that Lord Cockayne was a little shaky about the passing of time; it was perhaps something that might be called the telescoping of time that was shaking him in his turn. And Appleby felt that he had now been sufficiently perturbed; that, if possible, he ought to be, as it were, left gently toasting. Appleby glanced at his watch.

'I must find Cockayne, and take my leave,' he said. 'He has a touching faith in my detective powers, but it isn't really reasonable to expect much in the way of results after all these years. But I'm glad that you and I have had this chat. It really is curious that you should have been on the periphery of quite a bunch of these affairs. But it has been over a considerable period of time, which makes the coincidence we were speaking of a good deal less striking.'

'Quite so.' Sansbury took a more confident puff at his pipe. It was nevertheless improbable – Appleby thought – that he could imagine it was more than a truce that was being declared.

'And, of course,' Appleby pursued, 'I came in on Cockayne's ancient problem only in the most casual way. I believe I mentioned it to you at our first meeting. His youngest son is an acquaintance of my youngest son.'

'Ah, yes – Oswyn. A nice lad. They are at Oxford together?'

'Oh, no.' Appleby's tone was entirely indifferent. 'My boy is at Cambridge. He has heard some of your lectures, if I may mention the fact, with great satisfaction. He and Oswyn Lyward were simply at the same prep school.'

Chapter Seventeen

Mr Patrick Moyle (distinguished authority on practical jokes) and Mr Robert Appleby (scrum-half, retired) were both shortly to address themselves to the Final Honour School of *Literae Humaniores*. It might therefore be expected that, when confabulating together in the latter's digs in Holywell, the topic engrossing them would be – such is the curious constitution of that celebrated Oxford curriculum – either very ancient history or very modern philosophy.

But at the moment this seemed not to be the case. Signs of Bobby's studious disposition, indeed, were thick on the ground – literally so in the form of books rapidly consulted and then tossed ungratefully on the floor, crumpled notes, abandoned cups of black coffee, tumbled ash-trays, empty gin-bottles, half-gnawed bars of chocolate, and sundry other common indications of undergraduate addiction to learning. But for the moment, at least, neither young man appeared to have provided himself with useful employment of any sort. Mr Moyle was lying supine on the carpet, softly whistling to the ceiling. Now and then he would vary this posture and pastime by turning over on his tummy and cocking either a foot or a grotesquely clutching hand in air – the idea being to suggest that he was the worsted party in some desperate gunfight, and now *in articulo mortis*. Mr Appleby, properly enough, was paying no attention to this childish mime; instead, he prowled moodily about the room, and every now and then stuck his head out of the window, uttered an exclamation of gloomy impatience, and flung himself on a sofa before at once jumping up again and resuming his perambulation. Presently he varied this routine by going over to Mr Moyle and digging a toe hard into his ribs.

'You beetle off!' Mr Moyle said indignantly.

'You want attention, don't you? And I'm simply seeing if

you're a stiff yet. I don't believe you are. So here's to make sure.' Bobby engaged in motions suggestive of spraying Mr Moyle with bullets from some automatic weapon. 'Paddy,' he said – suddenly forgetting about this – 'you don't think Oswyn will have made a muck of it? I told my father he was to be relied on.'

'So he is, I think.' Paddy Moyle sat up. 'Oswyn's virtually decerebrate, of course. But he possesses that aristocratic *je ne sais quoi* that brings things off. I shouldn't be a bit surprised if he gets a degree. In Agriculture, isn't it? I'm told the hen-merchants are particularly susceptible to blue blood. Anyway, they do degrees on the battery-system, no doubt.'

'I don't care twopence whether Oswyn gets some ludicrous degree. I just want to know –' Bobby broke off to perform his ritual at the window. But Holywell was deserted. 'Is he driving back?'

'I suppose so.'

'Then he's probably in an ambulance – or already in a morgue. Or he's been nabbed for speeding.'

'Dicks don't nab lords.'

'Absolute rot!' Bobby was most indignant. 'They booked a duke only a couple of weeks ago.'

'Do you think your dad is going to book a marquis or a baron or a baronet, Bobby? Or will it just be a plebeian professor?'

'It won't be anybody at all, if Oswyn's made an ass of himself.' Bobby swung round. 'But there he is.'

It was certainly the peculiarly hideous horn on Oswyn Lyward's car which had sounded – very incongruously – from the direction of the Holywell Music Room. And a moment later there was a screech of brakes and the bang of a door thrust cheerfully open and shut again.

'You can tell he doesn't *think* he's made an ass of himself,' Paddy Moyle said encouragingly.

'Hullo, chaps.' Oswyn – who, like Bobby, made an instinctive ducking motion in going through anything other than an out-size in doorways – was in the room. 'The bleatin' of the kid excites the tiger.'

'The biznai prospers?' Bobby demanded.

'It does. *Jamais j'ai gloaté comme je gloaterai aujourd'hui.*'

Paddy groaned. He regarded playing *Stalky & Co.* as extremely childish.

'The guest turned up?' he asked.

'He turned up all right. Guests always do at Keynes.'

'You remembered you weren't to be in too much of a hurry with your stuff?'

'Of course I did.'

'And to be light and allusive – not to plug the thing?'

'My dear learned idiot, all that is going to be my *métier*. A lifetime of finesse stretches ahead of me.'

'When Oswyn,' Bobby said pedantically, 'is an honest man sent to lie abroad for the good of his country.'

'I say, that's rather good. As a definition, I mean.' Oswyn was interested. 'Have you made it up?'

'One Sir Henry Wotton. He was also capable of more elevated sentiments.

> "How happy is he born and taught
>   That serveth not another's will;
>   Whose armour is his honest thought,
>   And simple truth his utmost skill."

Moreover –'

'You two shut up!' Paddy shouted. 'Incidentally, why should I be kept half in the dark, and fobbed off with this anonymous guest stuff? If almost all the Patriarchs are to be put on parade, we might at least be told –'

'Orders from H.Q.' Oswyn said briskly. 'To wit, Sir John Appleby. Yours not to reason why. That's left to Bobby and me, who *have* to know. If all those average young imbeciles were let in on the classified information –'

'O.K., O.K.' Paddy – who was now wandering round Bobby's room apparently in the vague hope of finding something to drink – made a resigned gesture. 'Ours but to do and die. Do you think, by the way, there might be a chance of that sort of development?' Paddy was suddenly hopeful. 'A real free-for-all, I mean. When desperate criminals are cornered –'

'Paddy's mind is filled with the imagination of violence,' Bobby said. 'Our young intellectual lives in a reverie of gangsterdom. You should have seen him a few minutes ago. I had to

159

shoot him up on the hearth-rug just to keep him quiet and happy. As for the criminals, they're not desperate, at all. And high-class tricksters don't pull guns on you.'

'You ought to know.' Paddy was disappointed. 'Is there a whole bevy of them?'

'Your guess is about as good as mine. It may be a matter of a closely integrated team. Or there may just be a master-mind, plus some stooges and front men and fall guys.'

'Our Robert,' Paddy said, 'is not his father's son. He gets the terminology muddled. But never mind. This thing is on? Oswyn, you came away from home feeling it will be on?'

'No reason why it shouldn't be. But it depends on what may be called the improvisation factor. The quarry has to be jumped or bounced into it. They have to make a snap decision whether or not to go ahead. Are they prepared to play on those terms? That's the question. Bobby – wouldn't you say?'

'It's something like that. And there are adverse factors. The record so far suggests deliberation and careful planning, with long latent periods between operations. But they may go into action on an opportunist basis from time to time.'

'Why not *give* them more time?' Paddy asked.

'Because they might smell out a rat, I imagine. As I say, it's bouncing or nothing.'

'Mayn't they –'

'Or he. We just don't know.'

'All right. Mayn't he smell a rat already? About this place, for instance, and its harbouring Appleby *fils*?'

'That's one of the hazards,' Bobby said. 'But Appleby *père* has cracked down on his Oxonian son pretty hard. I had to hitch-hike half across England as a result.'

'It must be so bracing to have an absolutely ruthless daddy.' Mr Moyle, whose contribution to the debate had been made from his favourite position flat on the floor, suddenly sat up. 'I say,' he said. 'Talking about daddies. What if the villain turns out to be Oswyn's daddy? Will he have to be tried by the House of Lords?'

'My father is a little past affairs of this sort.' Oswyn spoke casually, but with a dangerous glance.

'Paddy's father,' Bobby said hastily, 'under the pretence

of keeping a bawdy-house, is a receiver of stolen goods. Shall we go out and get some lunch?'

'On the river somewhere.' Paddy scrambled to his feet. 'My confidence in all Lywards is absolute. I'm even prepared to go in Oswyn's lethal car.'

'The Trout,' said Oswyn.

'The Perch,' Bobby said.

'The Rose Revived,' Paddy said. 'But I'm prepared to toss for it. And for paying, as well.'

Tossing up between three people always takes a little working out, and the young men addressed themselves to the operation with gravity.

'Was there just one tiger?' Paddy asked Oswyn suddenly, when the issue had been determined.

'What do you mean?'

'At this lunch at Keynes yesterday. Did the kid – which I suppose was you – do his bleating to excite just one tiger, or several of them?'

'That would be telling,' Oswyn said. 'You'll be well briefed later.'

The Master looked with approval at the two silver tankards on his table, and at the bread and butter and cheese.

'Commons,' he said. 'As you very well remember, forty years ago nobody had anything else. Or not unless they were giving a luncheon party of a consciously extravagant kind. This was what your scout brought to your rooms, and this is what you ate and drank with entire satisfaction six or seven days a week for eight weeks on end.'

'And now?' Appleby asked.

'Unless they keep clear of college fare altogether, they huddle into hall and are given what is called a cooked meal. Two courses, three courses – I don't really know. But the appalling fact is that the change is in the interest of economy. Commons would cost more than concoctions do. The young *élite* of England, my dear Appleby, literally can't afford bread and cheese and beer. The luxury is reserved for Heads of Houses on their off days. Please help yourself.'

Appleby helped himself. It was clear to him that the Master

was a little dubious about what might be called the Appleby Plan. Hence this temporizing conversation. Which must be responded to.

'Just on your off days?' he asked.

'Yes, indeed. I lunch three young men, four days a week. That gets me through the whole lot, once in the academic year. But they'd be hurt in their minds if I gave them bread and cheese. Simple lads for the most part, you know, accustomed to Mum's good home cooking.'

'Bobby is accustomed to that,' Appleby said. The Master's social assumptions didn't entirely charm him. 'But he'd consider himself pretty well done by if he got cheese like this.' Appleby carved himself another chunk. 'A dozen juvenile guests a week makes quite an assignment. How do you get rid of them? I'm sure they're too nervous to rise and take their leave?'

'Perfectly true. I simply get up and shake hands. The brighter realize that the proceedings are terminated. Of course, they get back on me.'

'Get back on you?'

'They circulate the story that I have a formula.' The Master chuckled. 'I'm said to get to my feet and say, "That is all, thank you, at this stage".' The Master's chuckle suddenly became an engaging laugh. 'I must once have said it to some youth who was sent up to me for a wigging. Could any words be more idiotic? "That is all, thank you, at this stage." It's a fair cop. But, talking of lunches' – the Master took a plunge – 'do you reckon young Lyward will have brought it off at Keynes yesterday?'

'Lord, yes. It was on his home ground. And he's an extremely astute young man.'

'Perfectly true. It's in the family. I expect that even old Cockayne was sharp enough in his day. If all has gone well there, we must clear the decks for action, I suppose.'

'If you don't quite like it, Master, we can still rub it out.'

'Nothing of the kind. It means a certain amount of publicity, no doubt. But the college can stand that. Not but that some of the Fellows will make a row about it at a college meeting. Bad for our image, or something of the sort. Stupid catch phrase.'

'But so much the better, Master. The supposed dreadfulness

of publicity is the heart of the matter. The Governing Body of your college would rather resign itself to the thing vanishing without trace, than make a fuss about it in these particular circumstances. Both the disputed ownership, I mean, and the object's indubitable semi-sacred character.'

'Precisely so. It's all highly absurd, is it not?' This reflection seemed to have the effect of cheering up the Master quite a lot. 'It's only a year or two ago that I remember a colleague of mine reading rather an amusing paper to a dining club. He called it "College Treasures". It was about all the white elephants that such places get landed with – usually through the misconceived testamentary benevolence of old members. My own opinion has always been that the less a learned society gives the impression of being a museum the better. If I had my way, we'd sell all our blessed pictures and what not, and spend the money fifty fifty on central heating and research.'

'You have a reputation, Master, for radical thinking.'

'You flatter me, my dear chap.' The Master glanced with amused suspicion at Appleby. 'But did I tell you how the dispute over ownership came about? We have a traditional feud, as you know, with our immediate neighbours. Or at least the young men have. There are japes and jokes and raids and forays from time to time. Occasionally there's a certain amount of amusement in them, but I think I'd call it a tedious idea on the whole. Now, this dread receptacle –'

'An excellent phrase for it.'

'The novelist Richardson's, I think, in *Clarissa*. This dread receptacle is believed by some to have started the whole trouble. It was dug up – or, rather, uncovered, since it hadn't actually been buried – more or less athwart the boundary line. You follow me? Half within their curtilage, and half within ours.'

'A learned word, curtilage. How did it come about?'

'I imagine that some former Master, of rural inclination – or some similarly minded President, next door –'

'It is necessary to keep an open mind.'

'Precisely. One or other of these Heads of a House, a ripe scholar in the eighteenth century manner, was interested in keeping, say, pigs. So he used this piece of ancient junk as a trough. Then, in the earlier nineteenth century, somebody – say the

Prince Consort – invented an Improved Mechanical Feeder for pigs. So this affair got tossed aside – and nobody bothered that it lay half and half on our ground and theirs. Those were easygoing times.' The Master put a certain effect of nostalgia into this generalization. 'More cheese? No? Have an apple.'

Appleby took an apple. An antique stone sarcophagus, he was thinking, was an odd sort of apple of discord to have been pitched between two Oxford colleges.

'And then?' he asked.

'And then you are to imagine *our* chaplain and *their* Classics tutor taking the air together. It is a perfectly friendly stroll, and they are discussing some learned matter popular at the time: say, the problem of the historical Socrates. They come to a spot at which, on the boundary between the gardens of their respective colleges, some small repair or innovation is taking place. A drain is being laid, a wall rebuilt. The workmen intermit their labours and stand respectfully still as the gentlemen approach – which was quite the custom in Victorian Oxford, I may say. The scholars pause, for they are good Victorians too, and acknowledge a duty to offer an affable but at the same time edifying observation or two to these humble persons – who belong, you understand, to the respectable class of the Industrious Poor. Then, simultaneously, the eyes of each fall upon an object from which some pile of rubbish has just been cleared away. It is a time at which both Classical Archaeology and Christian Iconography have been making great strides. Within a couple of minutes our two friends know what they have discovered: a Roman sarcophagus which has been roughly adapted for the purpose of Christian sepulchre. The head of Hercules, for example, has been given a nimbus. It is all extremely interesting.'

'And so its ownership became a matter of prolonged dispute?'

'Yes, indeed. Indescribable animosities were generated, and at one point it was judged that the matter must be referred to the Judicial Committee of the Privy Council. But fortunately our respective Visitors intervened. The Visitor of a college, as you know, is some outside notability – an archbishop or the like – who can be appealed to for the purpose of settling internal disputes. So the matter of the sarcophagus was referred to the two Visitors jointly. It appears to me very improbable that they did more than meet over a drink and spin a coin to settle the matter. Anyway, the dread receptacle, I'm sorry to say, came to us. It's been a mild nuisance, you see, ever since. There was a previous occasion upon which the young men played some prank with it – after which we locked it up pretty securely. As you'll have noticed when I showed you the thing, there are places in which the adaptation to the purposes of medieval piety have been rather quaintly carried out.'

'And modern piety might be a good deal offended if it were frolicked around with?'

'Oh, most decidedly. People would write to the newspapers denouncing our young men for bad taste and moral depravity and heaven knows what. Any well-informed person could guess that we would go a long way to hush up anything of the kind – including quietly saying good-bye to this particular white elephant.'

'Even although it is now very valuable?'

'It hasn't much value to us. We don't much care for it – and, at the same time, I doubt whether we could sell it without raising some stupid outcry.' The Master finished his beer. 'The trouble about flogging anything of the kind nowadays is that it's invariably bought by some American. And then there's a shindy about letting priceless chunks of our cultural heritage leave the country. All worked up by fellows on fourpenny papers, who wouldn't know a chunk of cultural heritage from a chunk of cheese.'

For a moment Appleby had been lost in thought, but his attention appeared to be recaptured by the Master's last words.

'Cheese?' he said. 'Everything confirms me in the view that we have the finest chunk of cheese imaginable.'

'I'm glad you enjoyed it.' The Master sounded a shade surprised. 'Double Gloucester, I think.'

'It's very good indeed. But I was speaking metaphorically, as a matter of fact.'

'Dense of me. You think you've really got what will bait your trap?'

'Certainly I do. You've heard what I call the formula in these episodes: theft amid circumstances of disabling embarrassment

165

– together with a positive attraction to the freakish or bizarre. I decline to believe that your sarcophagus, once known about, is to be resisted. Or not in the light of what' – Appleby paused for a phrase – 'purports to be planned for it.'

'Which is quite something. I suppose it was your boy who told you about our dubious college treasure. Is it he who has thought up this monstrous joke as well?'

'Talk of Bobby's from time to time may be said to have furnished the materials. I've rather done the stringing of them together myself. About this railway-station business, by the way. Has it actually happened in recent times?'

'Recent times? It was essentially a pre-Kaiser's-War joke, of course. That sort of organized rag has rather gone out.'

'So the Patriarchs were concluding at their last dinner.'

'But it was brought off in a modified form a year or two ago. I don't recall what college the young man came from, or why he was being sent down. It must have been for some outrageous defiance of authority, or he wouldn't have been packed off for keeps. On the other hand, it can't have been for anything decidedly not on, because in that case the other men wouldn't have played, I imagine. They got hold of a coffin, easily enough. No doubt you can now buy such things in a supermarket, and simply walk out with it. But then they had to make do with somebody's car, because they couldn't get hold of a hearse. In the old days, a hearse would have been the prescriptive thing. The tradespeople, of course, were readier to indulge the young gentlemen in their whims.'

'I suppose so. But we must certainly have a hearse, Master. Your influence will be required.'

'Appleby, I am a timid man, and I have misgivings.'

'I don't believe it. And remember we are going to put a nail in the coffin of outrageous crime.'

'At least you won't put a nail in *our* coffin.' The Master chuckled as he rose from table. 'It's solid stone.'

Chapter Eighteen

'Have you heard about Paddy Moyle?' The question was fired by Bobby Appleby at the first person he came across in the Junior Common Room. 'The Master has sent him down.'

'Good Lord! Rusticated him, do you mean?'

'Nothing of the sort. Poor old Paddy is sacked for keeps.'

'Whatever for?'

'Atrocious immoralities. He was found in the chaplain's bed-room in the embraces of an enormous Negress. Paddy thought it was a fine and private place for embracing.'

'But that's monstrous!' A second young man had joined in, and it might have been possible to suppose that his voice was choked with emotion. This was occasioned, however, merely by his not having paused to finish the mastication of a slab of an-chovy toast. 'What's wrong with a Negress – even an enormous one? It's ghastly racial prejudice. The Master must be denoun-ced. There must be demonstrations and things. They have them regularly in all universities that are in the slightest degree with it. The trouble about Oxford is, you know, that it just isn't com-mitted.'

'But can we be sure' – a third and serious youth asked – 'that the Master wouldn't have acted in the same way if Pad-dy's amour had been with an equally enormous blonde Swede? Not that, in either case, it has anything to do with him. What's he hired for, really? To see the dons do their job. And what are *they* hired for? To shove us through exams. Not to bleeding well Eric-or-Little-by-Little us.'

'Perfectly true,' Bobby said, '– and I'm glad to see you know your *Stalky*.'

'There should be a special J.C.R. meeting,' the first young man said. 'Bobby – don't you think?'

'Well, I think we've thought of something better, as a matter of fact.'

'Who's "we"?'

'Just an obscure college society. Called the Patriarchs.' Bobby spoke tactfully, as to one beyond an indefinable pale. 'Paddy happened to read a paper to it not long ago. On rags and practical jokes. Paddy's a great authority on that sort of thing. So we're going to hold a rag in his honour. A going-down funeral.'

'What on earth is that?'

'It's the traditional thing when a chap is sent down – only it has fallen a bit into abeyance. You have a hearse and a coffin and mourners, and you do a grand funeral procession to the railway-station.'

'I see.' The serious youth didn't sound too enthusiastic. 'Don't you think that sort of elaborate joke tends to turn out un-funny?'

'It depends on how well it's mounted.' Bobby said this with marked firmness, since the objection was one to which, in other circumstances, he might have subscribed himself. 'I suppose you've heard of the Lewis and Short Sarcophagus?'

'I'm quite sure I haven't. It sounds absolutely idiotic.'

'You oughtn't to be so ignorant of the history of your own college. Lewis and Short were two dons: one of them here, and one of them next door. They came on this sarcophagus – which is a kind of stone coffin favoured by the ancient peoples – bang between the two colleges, so that there was a tremendous row about its ownership. But we have it now. It's locked up in that little place behind the chapel, and the S.C.R. tends to keep quiet about it. It's what's called a Christianized object. The pagan bas-reliefs on it have been –'

'Do be relevant,' the serious youth said impatiently. 'What's the point about this thing?'

'I'd have thought that pretty clear to the dimmest,' Bobby said politely. 'We're going to liberate it, and shove Paddy in it, and take him to the station that way.'

'In a hearse?'

'Certainly in a hearse. Hiring it has been a shade tricky. But there was a string we knew how to pull.'

'Is Paddy going to *lie* in this sarcophagus thing?'

'He must please himself. It's his funeral. I think he'll probably sit up.'

'I'm not sure the whole affair won't offend the religious susceptibilities of the citizens.'

'But that's bang in the picture, isn't it?' With a great effect of demagogic fervour, Bobby glanced round what was now quite a considerable auditory. 'The proposal is for a rag in the old-fashioned sense. But it's also a serious demonstration against arbitrary and obscurantist authority.' He paused long enough to remark that this ingenious double appeal had made a satisfactory impact. 'Any questions?'

'What happens at the railway-station?' somebody asked. 'Does this Moyle person simply climb out of his sarcophagus and shamble into a second-class compartment for Paddington? It sounds rather anti-climactic.'

'That's what used to happen – and it was rather a limp ending, I agree. But we've pulled another string. We're going to have a sombre van.'

'What the deuce is a sombre van?'

'It's something Oswyn Lyward found out about from an authority on such matters. It seems the railway companies used to do quite a trade in long-distance funerals, and that appropriate rolling-stock was available. You run across it, as a matter of fact, in Victorian novels.'

'*A Pair of Blue Eyes*.' An obscure youth – presumably reading English – spoke from the back of the crowd. 'Thomas Hardy. Two chaps are travelling on the same train, and intending to propose marriage to the same girl. They notice "a curious carriage, rich and solemn rather than gloomy in aspect" –'

'Quote, unquote,' somebody said disgustedly. 'It contains the girl's corpse, I suppose. Lay off. Bobby, go on.'

'It seems British Railways still have a few in running order. And we've managed to book one. Paddy – sarcophagus and all – will glide out of Oxford in his own private sombre van. When he gets to Didcot he can please himself. Don't you call that doing the thing in style?'

Murmurs of approval and appreciation greeted this appeal. The proposed rag had begun to take on an enticing elegance.

'Are there to be floral tributes?' somebody asked. 'Or is it No Flowers by Request?'

'Details later,' Bobby said. 'Just stand by for further orders.'

'Do you mean to say,' Judith Appleby asked her husband, 'that you have actually made the Master a party to this absurd plot? You've persuaded him to go through a form of sending Bobby's friend Paddy Moyle down?'

'Not exactly.' Appleby had made a brief return to Dream, but was displaying a reluctance to move out of earshot of the telephone. 'These boys aren't going to go and check up with the Master. Bobby simply wanders round murmuring "Paddy's being sent down, poor bastard", and everybody takes it for gospel. But, of course, I couldn't keep the Master in the dark – particularly as the plan involves borrowing valuable college property. So I've enlisted him as an ally. Or call it a sleeping partner.'

'Has it occurred to you that your precious sarcophagus –'

'Messrs Lewis and Short's precious sarcophagus.'

'Very well. That it's uncommonly like Lord Canadine's garden ornament?'

'So it is. So what?'

'The criminal may be chary of having rather a similar go twice.'

'I don't think so. It's just too tempting – the sarcophagus. Bobby calls it the bleating of the kid that –'

'Yes, I know. John, aren't you a little uneasy before this concept of light-hearted crime?'

'Uneasy?' For a moment Appleby considered. 'I'm not sure that I'm not. Put it that way.'

'All these affairs tend to take their colour in our minds from the first of them – or the first of them that we know about. The episode at Keynes Court was almost witty, and puts one in a kind of good humour with the whole series. But a Duccio is a Duccio –'

'Certainly it is. Has it occurred to you, Judith, that the Keynes Court business *may* have been a straight joke; that the perpetrators hadn't a clue as to the value of the small object they'd made off with; and that when the truth was revealed to them they were carried away by vistas of future affluence?'

'It's possible, I suppose. It has been the large-scale affair, so far as the brute number of impostors was concerned. A police escort, and Lord knows what. To me, that *does* suggest fun rather than crime. But it's a mere conjecture. By the way, have you thought enough about the lady in the case? There seems to be only one.'

'If you mean the august personage, I don't expect ever to meet her.'

'Nor do I. It's my guess that she was Sir Thomas Carrington's late mama. Sir Thomas is a very good suspect as the mastermind. His mother's talent as a painter set him going. And his Stubbs never was a Stubbs. It's his supposed loss that is what you call the bogus link – the one the criminal planted on himself by way of averting suspicion.'

'I'd like to believe so ingenious a notion. But the august personage is as likely to have been the capable Mrs Meatyard, or your obsessively gardening friend, Lady Canadine. But when one thinks about it, of course, it's clear that she must have been a professional actress of approximately the right age. Nobody else could possibly have carried out a successful impersonation of a public figure in that way – not even before such guileless people as the Cockaynes seem to have been. She's dead by now, more likely than not. And certainly *she* may have supposed herself to be involved only in an innocent joke. She'd have been told that the exploit was in the interest of a wager, or something like that. Indeed, in all these affairs it seems likely that most of the subsidiary figures could get away with a plea that they'd been ignorant of anything except fun and games as being involved. Which is why it's important – Ah, there it goes!'

The telephone had rung in another room, and Appleby hurried out. It was some minutes before he returned, and Judith gave the time to carrying a little further some mild research which she had been carrying on into Roman sarcophagi. What chiefly struck her was that such objects must be enormously heavy. She wondered whether the young men whom John was encouraging to such disorderly courses had very carefully thought out the mere mechanics of their operation. It was certainly likely that the thief – if thief there was going to be

– had efficiently thought out his. In none of his known depredations was there any record of a technical hitch.

'It's on!' Her husband was in the room again, boyishly triumphant. He might have been Bobby.

'Then, so far, so good.' Judith didn't fail to hear a certain lack of spontaneity in her own voice, but she couldn't quite identify what prompted it. It wasn't exactly that she hadn't wanted to play. Her encounter with the Canadines at Netherway had amused her very much; it had pleased her that Bobby had clearly shown resource at Sir Thomas Carrington's Monks Amble; she hadn't affected to be other than absorbed by John's accounts of the Meatyards, and Praxiteles, and her old friend Hildebert Braunkopf. It had all been, so far, very entertainingly a family affair. But she somehow distrusted the final absurdity to which it seemed to be building up. 'But how do you know?' she asked. 'Has something happened?'

'It certainly has. That was the Master on the telephone. The tiger has taken a first nibble – or at least has whisked his tail. The kid hasn't bleated in vain.'

'An identifiable tiger?'

'Say, an identifiable jackal. In fact, our Cambridge friend.'

'Sansbury? He's put in another of his appearances on the fringe of the affair? He must be off his head.'

'He doesn't strike me as that. But you may certainly judge his behaviour odd. After my second meeting with him – the one at Keynes Court – he can't but have been alerted and alarmed. Yet here he is – taking a couple of steps out of the wings, as it were, and making a little bow.'

'Just what kind of bow?'

'He rang up the Master, announced his name and standing, and said he had a colleague coming over from America some time in the fall. The colleague is interested in sarcophagi, and Sansbury is doing a little preliminary field-work for him. He'd heard of Lewis and Short, and wanted to check that it was still in the possession of the college, and that it would be available for inspection by a properly accredited scholar in a few months' time.'

'It doesn't make sense.'

'It certainly makes sense – up to a point. He was making sure that, tomorrow afternoon, labour and ingenuity weren't going to be lavished on the situation to no purpose. The young men might have got their facts all wrong, and be proposing to fool around with what was no more than a stone cattle-trough.'

'I can see that. But why on earth should Professor Sansbury make this inquiry in his own name? He'd have just got the same information from the Master if he'd put on an American accent and called himself Professor Töpperwein or Dr Deutschbein.'

'Perfectly true. And the explanation is obvious. He's between the devil and the deep blue sea, and no longer his own master.'

Chapter Nineteen

The obsequies of Paddy Moyle were to get a little out of hand in the end, but in their initial stages the organization at work could hardly have been faulted. For one thing, it was an organization that concealed itself, so that a marked effect of spontaneous extravagance was achieved. The Patriarchs, being a modestly exclusive club, had a flair for self-effacement, and it would have been difficult even for a pertinacious reporter from a London newspaper to discover just who had launched the spectacle. And 'spectacle' was certainly the appropriate word for these surprising *pompes funèbres*. The *cortège* which wound its way down the gentle and dreaming curve of the High was of a gratifying length. It was generally felt, moreover, that the mourners were as respectable as they were numerous; for although few appeared at all far advanced within the vale of years, the assemblage was yet highly representative of the athletic, social, and intellectual life of juvenile Oxford. Elderly and sentimental dons, drawn to a halt on the pavement by Mr Moyle's passing, murmured happily to themselves (with the poet Wordsworth) of so wide and fair a congregation in its budding-time of health and hope and beauty.

Nor was the occasion embarrassed by any officious appearance of the representatives of a narrow and restrictive conception of law and order. The Proctors were invisible: doubtless they were somewhere drowsed in burgundy and port. The Chief Constable quite failed to emerge from the Police Station, and his representatives in the streets gazed with an undisturbed equanimity at what was presumably but one more movie company concerned to create an authentic evocation of Oxford life. The citizenry came happily to the doors of their shops and booths to watch with smiling gratification what was essentially a memorial of better days, when the young scholars of the university were more abundant both in *joie de vivre* and (what so often conduces to it) ready money.

Many remarked on the richness, and some on the curiosity, of Mr Moyle's sepulchral casket. It was stone-coloured – and those who pressed near were able to determine that it was actually made of stone. It was ornamented in a deep relief: on one side, a *mêlée* of Romans and Orientals had been roughly adapted so as to afford a lively representation of the torments of the damned; on the other, a Last Judgement had been contrived from what might originally have been a scene in a Roman law-court. The lid (which had been found not quite to fit, and which must have been carved for purposes quite other than funerary ones) depicted some sort of Bacchic orgy; it lay beside the sarcophagus – in which Mr Moyle, still defiantly dressed in his scholar's gown, sat as if in an outlandish bath, sweepingly acknowledging with his academic cap alike the plaudits and the jeers of the bystanders.

Yet most voices were mute, so dumbfounding was the scene. Even the traffic stilled, and it might have been in a solemn silence that the procession wound its farther way but for the fact that Oxford is a bell-swarmed and towery city. It was as the hearse came abreast of the church of St Mary the Virgin, stolidly gazed upon from across the way by the effigy of the late Mr Cecil Rhodes, that a clamorous yet appositely mournful tintinnabulation broke out in every quarter of the sacred town. St Mary's itself has a big bell; Christ Church has a very big bell; all the little colleges (except perhaps the very newest ones) have little bells. And, in a single instant, all the bells began to toll. It was a memorable instance, long to be talked of in senior common rooms with envy and awe, of the stealth, the cunning, and the disinterested outrageousness of the young.

But youth, virtually resistless though it be, must sometimes suffer check. And that something of the kind had occurred became apparent when the procession reached Carfax. The person who approaches this celebrated *carrefour* from the High Street will reach the railway station by continuing straight ahead; if he turns right he will eventually find himself somewhere in the north of England; the left-hand road – named after that St Aldate of whom nothing whatever is known by anybody – will bring him quite soon to the River Thames (which has turned itself into the River Isis for the purpose of negotiating the purlieus of the university city). The procession, instead of continuing undiverted, turned down St Aldates. Having passed the Town Hall (on the steps of which the City Fathers stood aghast), it came upon another choice of routes. By turning right, it might reach St Ebbes (nothing whatever is known about St Ebba either). By turning left, it might enter Christ Church Meadow. It entered Christ Church Meadow.

The occasion of this change of plan was known to few. Such as it was, it appeared very simple. British Railways, willing to oblige with a Victorian sombre van for an authentic corpse, had turned awkward on somehow getting wind of the fact that the corpse was to be a spurious one. There was nothing surprising about this – or there would not have been to older persons, habituated to the general stuffiness of those who run large-scale public enterprises. As one Patriarch pointed out, the injunction to shed your cares by travelling by train would have received valuable reinforcement from the splendid publicity-value of Mr Moyle's funeral in the popular press. Nevertheless, British Railways had said No.

It is possible that the Patriarchs were here a little at fault in not having what is called contingency planning prepared. As it was, there had undeniably been a short period of dismay behind the scenes. Then somebody – it was significant that, later, nobody could quite remember who – suggested that Paddy's final passing could be turned into a kind of water-pageant. It could be in the manner of the *Morte Darthur*, with a barget (which presumably was a little barge) draped in black samite. Unfortunately samite turned out to be a rich silk fabric interwoven with gold. This sounded a shade daunting – whereupon somebody else urged a Viking funeral. This would be superior in itself, as being altogether more archetypal. A Ship of Death was the thing Long before Beowulf and all that crowd, the Etruscans had gone in for something of the sort, and there was a notable poem about it by D. H. Lawrence. You needed a great deal of fire, or at least a great deal of smoke. The blazing craft would drift down the Isis and vanish – no doubt with the corpse waving vigorously and cheerfully from the stern.

In the interest of this modest proposal (which remained a shade muddled, if the truth be told) various emergency arrangements were made. They had involved Bobby Appleby in a number of mysterious telephone calls. But, in the general excitement, nobody had taken much notice of that.

Christ Church Meadow is a quiet sort of place (a circumstance which has prompted some proponents of turmoil to propose building a motor-way across it). The citizens of Oxford eat their sandwiches in it, or perambulate it with their dogs. From time to time its secluded and pastoral character is emphasized by the appearance of some judiciously paraded cows. Young men in boating costume traverse it at a conscientious double as they go to and fro their aquatic occasions. It contains a Long and also a Broad Walk; and either of these, being wide and stately, is well accommodated to an occasional ceremonial purpose. It was such a purpose (although, it must be admitted, of a somewhat burlesque character) that was transacting itself now.

The Isis, when finally attained at the end of one of these vistas, presents, if in a modest and muddled way, what the English language, hot-foot after the American one, has come to call a marina. A variety of small craft, that is to say, are tied up, or anchored, or (whether manned or unmanned) appear simply to be drifting about. There are the river-cruisers of Mr Salter, which are really quite large, and which emphasize the fact by having names like *Majestic* painted pleasingly on their bows. There are all sorts of house-boats and motor-launches which, although it is intended that they should be confined to the south or farther bank, very understandably get in where they can. Not far off is the first of the few survivals of the stately college barges, once the centre of so brilliant a life during Eights Week and the like. And just as, in the huddled and roaring streets of Oxford, a maelstrom as they are of rubbery and shuddering buses and of gigantic 'articulated' commercial vehicles, the young men and women of the university continue recklessly to assert the absolute supremacy of their own intrepid bicycling selves, so here their slender and fragile craft – eights and fours and shells –

> Various vessels, moored in view,
> Skiff, gig, and cutter, or canoe –

manoeuvre with an equal disregard of modern hazards. It was to this spot (unfortunately) that the genius of the Patriarchs had finally conducted Mr Patrick Moyle and his coffin. Quite a lot of water (controlled however skilfully by the genius of the Thames Conservancy Board) was flowing down stream. Quite a lot of wind (controlled only by that same Providence to which the rapidity of Bobby Appleby's mental operations has been attributed in the opening paragraph of this sober chronicle) was blowing up stream. The water was therefore a little choppy.

The person of Bobby Appleby was now conducting itself with every appearance of slightly imbecile jollity. But equally it might have been said of Bobby that

> on his Front engraven
> Deliberation sat and publick care.

Bobby, like Satan, felt that there was a tricky operation on hand. The event – the almost immediate event – was to prove that this was so. Bobby felt, in these moments, that he could have done with the backing of Oswyn Lyward – of Oswyn whom he had lately permitted the comparatively guileless Paddy to describe as virtually decerebrate. But Oswyn, for good and sufficient reasons, was at present lying low. To be precise, he was lying low, together with Sir John Appleby and certain professional persons, in a police launch beneath the arch of Folly Bridge. Some fifty yards up stream, that was, from the extravagant events now gathering momentum before him.

Certainly the Ship of Death was in evidence. It had punctually appeared. It was even now being contemplated in mild perplexity by the President of Magdalen from above his enormous white beard. The President invariably took an afternoon stroll this way. But now the President strolled away again. And this was a fortunate issue of things for the President's peace of mind. For the beard of the venerable scholar might have turned yet more snowy had he been constrained to witness the alarming spectacle which at once succeeded.

The species of mortuary ritual now being simulated was, of course, that of a funeral pyre afloat. The dead warrior is put on board his ship; fire is applied to it; it drifts away blazing on the tide; finally it burns to the water and vanishes beneath the flood. Not quite all this, needless to say, was readily to be achieved on the Isis. But there was at least no difficulty in getting Paddy Moyle, together with his ponderous coffin and its equally ponderous lid, on board, for the Ship of Death (which appeared to be no more than a cabin cruiser appropriately dolled up) lay low on the water and there was very little heaving and shoving to do. Almost before the crowd was aware of what was happening – and there was now a considerable crowd on both banks of the river – the craft had cast off its moorings and glided towards the middle of the stream. All but the inner circle of the Patriarchs were plainly disconcerted by this. They had not purposed that Paddy should depart with only such maimed rites. There was, for example, to have been a poetic celebration of his career and lineage, delivered in a bardic manner by a young man – present and now in a state of high indignation – who had got himself up to look vaguely like a Druid. But at least there was nothing to complain about in the matter of the fire; it broke out instantly and to quite startling effect. Flames soared in air. There was an astonishing volume of smoke.

From either bank the younger sort produced a somewhat uncertain cheer. Presently these fireworks, as they must be, would extinguish themselves; the great cloud of smoke would be blown up stream; the absurd little craft would appear again; the rag would be over. Indeed, it was over already in the opinion of some, for people were already beginning to drift away from the river. But suddenly most of these were halted. For something odd had occurred.

The motor-boat (as it must soberly be called) had speeded up. It had so surprisingly speeded up as to have emerged, at least for a moment, from its own smoky penumbra. So there could not be the slightest doubt of what was at the moment transacting itself on board. Mr Patrick Moyle, treacherously and suddenly seized by somebody from behind, had been yanked out of his sarcophagus and pitched into the river. His features, strangely enough, were recorded by those nearest to the scene to have expressed – as he came to the surface and swam for the Oriel raft – neither annoyance nor surprise. Which was very strange. For it had been, after all, a scurvy fashion in which to treat a corpse.

And now there was pursuit. From beneath Folly Bridge flashed the police-launch containing Sir John Appleby. From out of the New Cut came a second launch, manned by purposeful employees of the Thames Conservancy Board. The escaping motor-boat roared down the Green Bank. It was a thousand pities that this was about all that the great majority of the assembled concourse saw. For the catastrophe took place half a mile farther on – beyond Long Bridges (where there is a bathing-place nowadays) and in the tricky stretch of water which rowing men know as the Gut.

The Gut is not what it was. It has been monkeyed with. But not to the extent of totally obviating all navigational hazards in its double curve. Those who had strolled down the tow-path thus far were to display a surprising unanimity in their testimony before the Oxford City Coroner. The fleeing motor-boat – clearly to be seen as manned by two elderly men – was cutting its corners in a dangerous way. This was to be expected of persons in an extravagant hurry. Anywhere but in the Gut, it might have mattered little. But just here, as it happens, one may have very little notice of some other craft, coming head-on upon an orthodox course. Such a craft appeared now. And it was the 'Varsity Boat!

The horror of this moment will not soon be forgotten by those who witnessed it. Here were the nine young men (for one ought never to ignore the cox) on whom the fortunes of the University of Oxford, *vis-à-vis* the University of Cambridge, solely depended in a few weeks' time. And bearing directly down upon them was the fugitive motor-boat, its character as a projectile enhanced by its notable burden of a massive stone sarcophagus, complete with lid, and understood by the learned to be carved in peperino stone and to date from the third century B.C. It is agreed by all that the motor-boat, had it roared on regardless of what it did, would have smashed the slender Oxford shell to matchwood, and doubtless hurled the dismembered limbs of its occupants down the hurrying Isis – as once the fragmented

Orpheus (another very handsome youth) down the even swifter Hebrus to the Lesbian shore.

This comprehensive calamity did not take place. For the elderly man at the wheel of the motor-boat, seeing the imminent peril, hurled his craft into a reckless arc. At this point the south bank of the Isis is solid concrete, three feet high. The motor-boat hit this glancingly, for its bows were already up in air. It somersaulted grotesquely amid flying spray, plunged into the river, and vanished. The Oxford stroke looked only at the cox's nose. The seven men behind him looked only at the back of the head of the man in front. This is called keeping one's eyes in the boat. The cox gave a single cold glance at the piece of nonsense which had thus troubled the water. Then, unperturbed and magnificent, the 'Varsity Boat rowed on. For good measure, the cox gave them ten. A bicycling figure on the tow-path, with a red face and a pink Leander scarf, bellowed at them encouragingly through a megaphone. Half a minute later the motor-boat surfaced, bottom up. Two or three humane persons, allowing themselves to be diverted from pounding along on foot behind Oxford's hope, started to run around looking for lifebuoys. They judged they would be useful when the crew of the motor-boat also surfaced.

But nobody surfaced. It was a full hour before the frog-men came. As dusk fell they discovered the bodies. Pinned beneath the sarcophagus and its lid respectively, Lord Canadine and Professor Sansbury (a Cambridge man) lay pinned in Isis ooze.

Chapter Twenty

'Awfully good of you to have come in and given me early word of the thing,' the Commissioner said. 'I suppose it will have repercussions here in due course.' The Commissioner was standing at his window gazing out over the Thames, now brown and broad and tidal, as it emerged beneath Westminster Bridge. 'A pity the Boat Race doesn't come as far down stream as this,' he said. 'One would get a nice view. Only it sounds as if, this year, there might have been no Boat Race at all.'

'Quite so – in which case the Applebys would not have been very popular. Judith says it ought to be a lesson to me.' Sir John Appleby paused thoughtfully. 'And I dare say she's right.'

'But she took a hand too, didn't she? And actually with Canadine himself.'

'Perfectly true. But she didn't encourage her own son to organize an extravagant and – as it turned out – lethal rag.'

'Ah, well.' The Commissioner, who seemed a little at a loss before this aspect of the matter, turned back to his desk. 'As I was saying, there will be repercussions here. Some of these defrauded people will come asking for their stolen property.'

'I hardly think they're likely to get it. Cockayne's Duccio and Carrington's Stubbs will by now be in private collections – very private collections – in the United States. Braunkopf is presumably to be deemed the legal owner of the Nanna and Pippa, and will no doubt part with it advantageously to some well-heeled art-lover quite soon. The Meatyards are unlikely to try to get some money back for "Autumn Woods". The Lewis and Short Sarcophagus is now home again in college, and will be all right after a good scrub up. As for Canadine's antique statue, it was never, of course, anything of the sort. There are places in Germany where you can commission gross objects of the kind, and that is probably what Canadine's father did.'

'My dear Appleby, I am curious. How did you come to pick out Canadine from, so to speak, the middle of all this nonsense?'

'It was partly what I've just been saying. A valuable antique statue for long leading an unregarded life as a garden ornament is a most implausible conception – as Judith felt at the start. Then Canadine was the only person who, when defrauded or practised upon, didn't, initially at least, make some public fuss. Canadine only told a few private friends. His little insurance policy, that is to say, was to remain confidential unless it was by any chance needed. He could at any time show that he belonged with the cheated, and so could hardly be regarded as the cheater.'

'It sounds a crackpot notion to me.'

'Certainly. But Canadine *was* a bit of a crack-pot. And he was the kind that gets fun out of *knowing* that he is. But you were asking me how I plumped for him. In the end, it was a matter of the most utterly primitive criminal investigation. He gave Judith a plan of his blessed railway, you know. Well, there – bang in the middle of it – was the vital fingerprint.'

'I've never heard of a twenty-year-old fingerprint. You must – yet once more, my dear fellow – have made criminological history. Canadine was the equerry in the bogus royal visit to Keynes?'

'Undoubtedly he was. He wasn't personally known to the Lywards at that time. The affair may well have been planned as a genuine joke – and then Canadine glimpsed that there was, as it were, a career in it.'

'I'm surprised he lasted so long. In this last business he appears to have been utterly reckless. How did you set him on it, anyway?'

'By having Cockayne ask him to lunch, and having Cockayne's youngest son, Oswyn, chatter about the rag he was organizing for his friend who was being sent down, and of the part to be played in it by the sarcophagus. A love of the really freakish was Canadine's Achilles heel, poor fellow. He fell for it instantly. And his organization was once more superb, you know. He was behind British Railways' withdrawing their agreement to provide a van. I suppose as an amateur of railways he had a pull with them. And look how he managed the funeral barge, or whatever it's to be called. He diverted the real one by a false

message to some wharf higher up the river. And there he was –
together with that wretched Sansbury – at the appointed spot
with his own.'

'How was he proposing to make his effective get-away?
Surely he'd have been held up at – what's it called? – Iffley Lock.'

'Ah, your Oxford topography isn't up to date.' Appleby chuckled. 'There's a bridge now, you see, half a mile short of that –
Donnington Bridge. It carries something like a whacking great
motor-way across the Isis. He had only to run ashore there,
have a lorry with a hoist waiting –'

'But he never made it. He had a shade too much respect for
young lives.' The Commissioner fiddled with a paper-weight.
'I'm bound to say, the fellow had a sense of style. A peer of the
realm in quod for that sort of thing would be awfully awkward.
Hardly fair on the screws.'

'I don't think he meant to commit suicide. He just took an
instantaneous big risk because he disliked the idea of man-
slaughter.'

'That's how one has to look at it, no doubt. And it was Sansbury who got the raw deal. In that second of crisis, he had no
say in the matter. He wasn't at the tiller. For that matter, he
wasn't at the tiller all through.'

'Indeed, he wasn't. A weak character, if ever there was one.
Plenty of cleverness, plenty of conceit. But he certainly got
shoved around. Or call it deeper and deeper in. For long, of
course, there was no single affair in which his part, viewed in
isolation, could not be interpreted as more or less innocent. He
was probably slow to see that the eventual addition sum, as one
may call it, would be damning. Canadine must have had some
ugly hold on him, to make him progressively expose himself as
he did. He had the role in a crisis of what Bobby calls the fall-
guy, poor devil '

'It wouldn't have saved Canadine.' The Commissioner appeared to recall that some civil inquiry should here be made.
'And how is Bobby? I hope this business won't upset him, so
shortly before those important final exams.'

'I don't think so.' Appleby glanced at his watch. 'As a matter
of fact he'll be waiting for me down below with the car.'

'You ought to have told him to come up.' But the Commissioner was looking at his watch too. 'Awfully good of you to have come in,' he said. 'We must have that lunch together soon. Get your secretary to ring up my secretary any time. My dear fellow, good-bye.'

'Shall we be put inside: Oswyn and Paddy and me?' As he piloted the Rover round Parliament Square, Bobby Appleby asked this question casually enough.

'Definitely not. And the odd thing is that *nobody* is likely to be put inside. In all these affairs, various minor villains must have been involved. But I don't think anybody's going to catch up with them.'

'Not you?'

'Decidedly not me.'

'Calling it a day, Daddy?'

'Just that.' The car was heading for the Great West Road, and Appleby was silent for the whole length of Victoria Street. 'Straight to college, I suppose,' he said. 'I drop you, and drive home.'

'Yes.'

'Give my regards to the Master, if you run across him in the quad.'

'Of course.'

'Your mother is likely to feel that the supervision of Hoobin, and the apple-trees, and my mythical apiculture –'

'What's that? Oh, bee-keeping, of course.'

'She is likely to feel that these should be my principal occupation for some time.'

'Yes,' Bobby said. 'I'm afraid that's true.'

More about Penguins

Penguinews, which appears every month, contains
details of all the new books issued by Penguins as
they are published. From time to time it is
supplemented by *Penguins in Print*, which is a
complete list of all available books published by
Penguins. (There are well over three thousand of these.)

A specimen copy of *Penguinews* will be sent to you
free on request, and you can become a subscriber
for the price of the postage. For a year's issues
(including the complete lists) please send 30p if you live in
the United Kingdom, or 60p if you live elsewhere. Just
write to Dept EP, Penguin Books Ltd, Harmondsworth,
Middlesex, enclosing a cheque or postal order, and your
name will be added to the mailing list.

Note: *Penguinews* and *Penguins in Print* are not
available in the U.S.A. or Canada

Raymond Chandler

Farewell, My Lovely

'The dialogue crackles, the killer kills, the action covers a
great deal of ground and hard knocks at terrific speed'
– *Spectator*

The High Window

'Very tough, very tense, enormously lively' – *Observer*

*Killer in the Rain**

Every one of these eight stories has the deadly Chandler *élan*.

The Lady in the Lake

'It is most efficiently written: the story travels at
exhilarating speed. It is a brilliant who-dun-it'
– Desmond MacCarthy in the *Sunday Times*

The Long Good-Bye

'Chandler is the most brilliant author now writing this
kind of story' – Somerset Maugham

Playback

Chandler's last great thriller

Trouble is my Business

A Penguin collection of short stories by the American
master of the tough thriller.

The Big Sleep

'A book to be read at a sitting' – *Sunday Times*

Pearls are a Nuisance

'Full of life and character: as tense as a tiger springing
into action' – *Daily Telegraph*

Smart Aleck Kill

A collection of four of his most hard-boiled short stories.

Not for sale in the U.S.A. or Canada
**Not for sale in the U.S.A. only*

Simenon Crime available in Penguins

Maigret Mystified

Murder in a quiet Paris square.

This is one of the earliest Maigrets, in which the
Inspector gradually uncovers a genteel underworld of old
jealousies and stifled hatreds in the mystifying case of
M. Couchet, shot dead in the office of his pharmaceutical
firm.

The Blue Room★

'Would you like to spend the rest of your life with me?'
'Of course.'

Tony would have given anything to wipe out that 'of
course' . . . two casual words which were to incriminate him
as the partner in a long-planned double murder, an
innocent man caught up in a nightmarish web of
circumstantial evidence.

Also available:

Maigret meets a Milord
Maigret and the Hundred Gibbets
Maigret and the Enigmatic Lett
Maigret has Scruples★
Maigret's First Case★
Maigret Loses His Temper★
The Iron Staircase★
Account Unsettled★

★Not for sale in the U.S.A. or Canada

JOHN DICKSON CARR

The Emperor's Snuff-Box

Everyone liked her . . . everyone was against her . . . so
they framed her.

Eve Neill should never have entertained a man in her
bedroom right opposite her fiancé's house. Especially a
violently jealous ex-husband with a savage temper and a
cunning plot to settle her hash for good. She should have
listened to what he said instead of pleading with him. That
way she could have avoided a murder charge.

Poison in Jest

He laughed as he died, but the laughter died with
him. Something had changed in the Quayle
household, up in the mountains. Clocks ticked,
floorboards creaked, and footsteps could be heard in
the hallway at night. Poison had taken up its
lodging. One of the family had turned murderer. . .

Also available:

The Dead Man's Knock
Hag's Nook*
The Mad Hatter Mystery
Till Death Do Us Part
The Witch of the Low Tide

Not for sale in the U.S.A. or Canada
**Not for sale in the U.S.A. only*

Michael Innes

'Mr Innes can write any other detective novelist out of sight. His books will stand reading again and again' – *Time and Tide*

'The most able writer of grotesque fantasy in crime fiction' – *Birmingham Post*

'A master – he constructs a plot that twists and turns like an electric eel: it gives you shock upon shock and you cannot let go' – *The Times Literary Supplement*

'The intellectual, the phantasmagoric, the exhilarating Mr Innes' – *Church Times*

The following Penguins by Michael Innes are available:

Appleby at Allington
Appleby's End
Appleby on Ararat
A Connoisseur's Case
The Daffodil Affair
Death at the Chase
The Long Farewell
Money from Holme
Night of Errors
Operation Pax
Secret Vanguard
Sonia Wayward
What Happened at Hazlewood

Not for sale in the U.S.A.